KILLER!

Azul powered to his feet, pitching the Mexican out and forwards at the far wall. The Winchester boomed. The man in the air screamed again as the bullet ripped through his body, shattering his left shoulder. He hit the floor and rolled over, groaning as he crawled towards his companion.

Azul dropped to the right, drawing his Colt as he fell.

A third rifle shot ploughed splinters from the woodwork behind him. He hit the floor and rolled, firing blind. The fat Mexican was on his feet, levering the rifle. Azul fired back. His bullet hit the man two inches below the bandoliers, just beneath the vee of his rib-cage. It tore through the soft spread of his belly, puncturing the stomach sac before blasting out through his spine . . .

Other BREED novels by James A. Muir in Sphere Books

THE LONELY HUNT
THE SILENT KILL
CRY FOR VENGEANCE
DEATH STAGE
THE GALLOWS TREE
THE JUDAS GOAT

BREED:
Time of The Wolf

JAMES A. MUIR

SPHERE BOOKS LIMITED
30/32 Gray's Inn Road, London WC1X 8JL

First published by Sphere Books Ltd 1978

Good memories are made of friendship and food,
so this one is for Giorgos and Christoforos Veneris.

Set in Intertype Times

Printed in Great Britain by
Hunt Barnard Printing Ltd.,
Aylesbury, Bucks

CHAPTER ONE

The timber wolf watched the man ride past with a cold, yellow gaze. It was a big animal, the heavy shoulders and powerful haunches bunching under its thick grey pelt, tensed even in repose. Its colouring blended into the mottled shading of stone and shadow and starlight so that it was almost invisible, and it halted the bone-crunching action of its massive jaws the instant it sensed the approach of man and horse. Stealth, as much as strength, had kept the wolf alive long enough to regard a man with calm respect.

A full-grown pronghorn stretched on the rock before the animal. The antelope's neck was broken, torn, and blood welled sluggishly from its ripped stomach cavity.

The wolf slid a long tongue gently over its fangs lapping blood from the curving teeth. The taste woke the hunger again – it had been some days since the last kill – and the great beast let a low, near-silent growl rumble from its chest, irritated by the need for caution. The succulent odour of the butchered antelope rose temptingly on the night air, but still the need for secrecy prevailed. The animal watched the man draw closer, instinct telling the creature that this was no hunter – not of wolves, not then – but man was still an enemy. Any man. The wolf sat silent, watching.

A nightjar screamed and the man stirred in his saddle, hiking his shoulders back as though easing muscles wearied by long hours of riding. He looked up, and moonlight played for a moment on yellow hair as pale blue eyes scanned the darkness.

The wolf watched. The rider drew level, and the big lobo hunched down closer to the ground, ready to contest his hard-won kill. The man rode slowly, letting his pony make its own pace. He rode with the reins held loose in his left hand. His right was on the saddlehorn, close to the butt of the Colt cross-hung around his waist.

The horse sensed the watcher and its ears flattened back along its angular skull. The man, too, sensed something in the night and his hand moved to rest lightly on his gun. His head lifted, listening. He grunted softly, urging the horse on past the wolf's position, sniffing the air like an animal.

The wolf held silence. The man went past. Still the wolf watched; watched until the horse was gone from sight amongst the trees and the nightjar settled down. For a while longer the lobo stayed alert, ears pricked and nostrils flared for hint of danger. The night grew quiet again.

After a while the wolf decided it was safe to eat. Saliva dribbled from its mouth and a low, anticipatory rumble echoed from deep inside its belly. It opened its jaws, darting its big, grey head forwards to burrow into the tasty belly sac of the dead pronghorn. The blood and the pungent intestines inflamed the lobo's appetite and it dragged its head back, gulping down a great mouthful of steaming viscera.

In seconds, the man was a dim memory, almost forgotten as the wolf settled to its feast.

The man rode on with a faint smile on his wide-lipped mouth. His memory was longer than the wolf's, but in most other ways his senses were much the same. He had smelled the sweet scent of fresh blood, had known that something watched him. And guessed that some other hunter had made a kill that night. Not a cougar, for one of the big cats would have warned him off with a snarl, too proud, too confident of its own strength to remain silent. Not a coyote, for that would have dragged its kill clear and run. A wolf then, and a solitary wolf at that.

The kind the Mexicans called *el lobo solitario* – a lone wolf like himself. He wished the animal joy of its kill. And wondered how long it might be before he made his.

He was a tall man, lean and muscular, slumping in the saddle with the deceptive grace of one accustomed to spending long hours on horseback. A wide-brimmed stetson shaded his face, a tangled spill of sun-bleached blond hair falling down his neck, almost to his shoulders. He wore a shirt of faded linen, washed enough that it was now almost colourless, and a waist-coat of supple, well-worn leather. His pants were buck-skin, worn and weathered like the rest of his clothes, tucked into a pair of moccasins that rose to just below his knees. They were laced at the front, Apache style, and from the right there protruded the hilt of a slender-bladed throwing knife. His gunbelt looked more cared for than his clothing. It sat snug about his narrow waist, the holster hitched round to the left for riding, the butt of a Colt's Frontier model sticking out where he could draw it fast. On the other side of the belt was a long, wide sheath holding a broad-bladed Bowie knife, the tang and guard shining bright in the moon's light.

All his weapons were clean and oiled, tended carefully, as though much used.

There was about him an air of controlled tension, much akin to that of the lobo, as if – for all his casual slump – he could power instantly to action.

His face was tanned and leanly planed, the cheek-bones and nose wider than was usual amongst European-descended Americans, the nose flattened slightly above the wide, full-lipped mouth. His eyes were narrowed by years of staring into sun-baked landscapes, and very blue. A woman would have thought him hand-some. And dangerous. A man would have settled for dangerous – and wondered at his ancestry, for there was about him a mixture of racial characteristics.

He was a half-breed, a *mestizo*. Like the wolf, a *lobo*.

He had been christened, in the cathedral in Santa Fe, Matthew Gunn. That had been his father's wish: that he be given a white name. His father had been called Kieron Gunn. His mother had been called Rainbow Hair, in the fashion of her Chiricahua people who had named him Azul, for his blue eyes.

Through his veins flowed the blood of his father's Scottish ancestors, mingling with the darker strain of his mother's people.

Around the Border territory he was called Breed.

And men feared him, for that latter name had come to mean something else: death.

He glanced up at the moon, calculating the hours until dawn. It was, he reckoned, only a little time off. That meant he should reach Tubac around mid-morning. From Tubac – where he hoped to pick up news – it was a day, maybe a day and a half, to Tucson. A long way to go to find one man. Unless that man had killed your parents and your people. That made the distance immaterial.

He shifted in the saddle, easing the stiffness. His Apache upbringing had taught him to ride for longer periods than most whitemen could manage, but thirty hours was still a long time. Even with halts to refresh the horse. Even for a Chiricahua warrior.

But word around the Border towns had it that Nolan was headed north, and if he hadn't split eastwards for El Paso or west towards Fort Yuma, the dark man would be making for Tucson. It was about the only place he could safely bank around seventy thousand dollars of stolen money. The only place he could hope to find a printer with the machinery to utilise two plates of metal, the kind of metal that prints five dollar bills stolen from a coffin.*

And Nolan was the man who had killed his parents. The man he hunted.

His horse was tired, close to faltering even though he allowed the beast to pick up its own speed. He swung out of the saddle, and walked, leading the animal. It could rest in Tubac. Or he could purchase a fresh

* See Breed 6 – The Judas Goat.

mount. He doubted that would be necessary: the big black was rangy and deep-chested, a mixture of mustang and thoroughbred that combined speed with staying power. A time of rest and decent eating would refresh them both, ready for the journey north.

He moved on at a steady pace; sure-footed even though halfway asleep himself.

Hate can do a lot for a man's resources.

When the sky got brighter he mounted again and walked the pony onwards through the pines. The light that was swelling up across the sky from the east outlined the stark branches of the big trees, the thicker configurations of the loblollies and the cedars. Birds began to chirrup a greeting and the downslopes of the Sierra Madre got noisy with animal life. Azul tugged a narrow stick of jerky from his belt and chewed as he rode on.

Somewhere behind him the wolf howled. It was a long, mournful sound, as if the lobo regretted the coming of the dawn.

He reached the flatlands stretching up from the Sierras to the southern slopes of the Colorado Plateau and urged the big black to a faster pace. The horse went forwards willingly, sensing the township ahead. Maybe guessing, in its animal mind, that it could rest up there.

The sun came up and the land flattened out, rock and pine giving way to sand and cactus and sparse, sun-yellowed grasslands. The southern branch of the San Pedro river spilled down across the cattlelands to his right, providing just enough water to make the prospect of ranching in the near-barren Arizona territory tempting enough – profitable enough – to be worthwhile to the *pinda-lick-oyi* ranchers filling up the territory.

He reined in alongside a little feeder stream and watered the pony. There was grass thrusting up through the arid soil and he let the horse crop while he washed his face and hands, drank himself. Then he mounted again and heeled the black to a canter, heading for Tubac.

The place was a straggle of baked adobe and bleached wood, a comingling of styles and races more mixed than his own blood.

A rutted wagon trail led into the town, passing through a cluster of wickiups and hogans built at a respectful – or nervous – distance from the single main street. The signs daubed on the lodges were faded and dirtied, like the Apaches he saw squatting in the dust outside them. He recognised the marks of Mimbreño and Jacarillo, some Ojo Caliente, and a sprinkling of Pima lodges.

He felt ashamed for those of his brothers who had chosen to give up the free life of Apacheria for the grubby existence of hand-outs and easy liquor to be found on the outskirts of a *pinda-lick-oyi* settlement.

The town itself – if town was the right description – was little better. Mainstreet was a wide avenue of baked sand, thick with horse droppings and garbage, rutted deep by wagons and stifling with the odour of frying food. There was a cantina and a saloon, both open and already doing business. The heaviest smell came from an eating house with a gold-painted sign announcing the Tubac Palace Restaurant as the finest eatery between Nogales and Tucson. There was a livery stable set back from the street and a spread of cattle pens off to the west side; empty and looking unused. In between were stores: two gunsmiths, a milliners, a general store, a hardware outfit. There was a dusty office claiming to be the local branch of the Arizona Territory Cattleman's Association, and a stage depot. They were both closed and the yellowed glass in the windows looked fly-blown and dirty. A *Panderia* was doing business, but apart from that and the saloons, the town felt sleepy and lazy and quiet.

He saw a lodging house called the Tubac Rest and reined in outside. Like the rest of the town the place was only one storey high and looked dirty.

He climbed down off the black horse and pulled his Winchester clear of the saddle boot. His feet sank down into the soft sand of the street's edges and he stamped up the steps, kicking dust from his moccasins.

An old man was sweeping the place out, lifting clouds of dust from a faded carpet and batting a gnarled hand at the flies buzzing irritably around his head. There were three bleached loungers set against the far wall and a scarred desk set in front of an alcove with pigeon-holes built into the adobe. Off to the right was a narrow restaurant where two Mexican women were serving coffee and eggs and bacon to a handful of residents.

Azul walked past the old man, slapping his stetson against his shirt and legs to add more dust to the oldster's task.

He put his carbine down on the desk and slapped the bell. The button went down, making a dull sound against the frame. He pushed the thing aside and slapped his hand on the desk. Nothing happened. He turned around, looking for the old man. There was a swirl of dust around the outside door, but no sign of the cleaner. He picked up his Winchester and dropped it noisily on to the cracked veneer.

'Hombre! Que pasar? Que quieren? Calmarsen!'

The voice was low and throaty. And unmistakably feminine. He spun round, his right hand dropping naturally towards his pistol.

'Ole! Pistolero, no es?' The woman stood just inside the frame of the dining-room door, smiling. *'Y que guapo! Que tenga que ver conmigo?'*

'A room,' said Azul. 'A room and a bath.'

He reached back, picking up the Winchester as the woman walked towards him. She was still smiling, her eyes running over his body in a way that made him feel slightly uneasy. She was big, nearly as tall as he, with a figure to match. It thrust out the tight material of her dark green dress, bulging up where the bodice was cut down over her breasts, spreading out from a trim waist into flowing lines that accentuated the sway of her wide hips. Her hair was of a dark brown, like burnt cork, emphasising the pale tan of her face; she looked like she saw little daylight.

Her features were solid, almost too big. A wide mouth devoid of colouring other than the natural redness of the full, fleshy lips. Two huge eyes, shaded with blue-grey mascara that hid beneath the shadow of long lashes. A wide, straight nose between high cheekbones akin to his own.

She held her head straight and proud on a long, slender neck, and he noticed that her hands were smooth and long and tipped with scarlet paint. He noticed, too, that she was beautiful. Not in any conventional sense, but in that kind of near-ugly loveliness that makes a man want to reach out and grab a woman without a thought for the consequences.

'So you want a room,' she murmured. 'For how long?'

'Depends,' said Azul. 'A night. Maybe longer.'

'Depends on what?' Her eyes fluttered over him like sensual butterflies. 'Are you looking for someone?'

Azul nodded: 'Yeah. A tall man, dressed all in black. He's got dark hair and green eyes. Looks mean. He might have spread money around.'

'So. A bounty hunter. *No es?*'

'No,' said Azul. 'This is private between him an' me.'

'I have not seen anyone like that,' murmured the woman, 'so perhaps you should stay around and ask some other people. Maybe someone in the saloon or the cantina has seen him.'

She opened a dusty register book and brushed a dead fly from between the pages. Dipping a wood pen into a cracked inkwell, she held the instrument in Azul's direction.

'Sign here, please. You can write?'

Azul grinned and signed his name. He had been taught to write by his father. He signed in as Matthew Gunn.

'It will be two dollars American.' She turned the book towards her as she spoke. 'A dollar extra for a hot bath.'

Then she gasped, her eyes getting even larger as she read the signature.

'*Madre de Dios!* You are the one they call Breed!'

'I heard it said,' grunted Azul. 'Does that make any difference?'

'No! No, of course not. You are welcome, *señor* Gunn. I shall attend to your bath myself.'

'Good,' he said. 'But first I'd like to sleep. Give me about four hours, then fix the bath. All right?'

'*Claro!* I shall see to it personally.'

Azul turned away, ignoring her wide-eyed wonder as he studied the number burned into the wooden tag attached to his key. He grinned when he saw that he occupied room thirteen.

'I'll be back in a while,' he said. 'I got to bed my horse down first.'

He canted the Winchester over his right shoulder, keeping his thumb on the hammer and his forefinger over the trigger as he pushed through the doors and tugged the reins free of the hitching post. Then he paced down the street to the stable, ignoring the curious stares of the townsfolk beginning to spill out into the dusty thoroughfare.

He walked the black down to the stable and handed over two dollars to the stableboy in return for a clean stall and a feed of grain. Another dollar bought a grooming and a bucket of fresh fodder. He left his saddle hooked over the rails: the bags held nothing worth stealing and the saddle itself was no better than any of the others he saw inside the barn.

The stableboy hadn't seen a dark man with green eyes either.

Back at the rooming house, the woman greeted him at the door.

'Your room is ready,' she smiled. 'I had it specially cleaned.'

'Thanks,' grunted Azul.

'By the way.' Her voice halted him at the entrance. 'My name is Linda. Linda Velazquez. *Viuda* Velazquez.'

The emphasis on the Mexican word for *widow* held a

lot of promise that didn't, just then, interest Azul very much.

'Sure,' he said. 'Thanks.'

He went inside and closed the door. There was no lock, but a hefty-looking bolt that he slid into the socket before going over to check the window. There was no glass, but twin shutters with moveable louvres to let air into the room. He pulled the shutters tight and dropped the cross-bar to close them, then adjusted the louvres just enough that air could drift in without allowing sufficient gap for clear sight into the room.

It was small, but relatively clean. The floor was made of bare wood planks with cracks showing where the timber had shrunk, the walls of whitewashed adobe. There was a big, wide bed, all brass head and tail boards with a hard mattress in between, sharp pieces of straw sticking up through the sheets. A washstand flanked the bed, holding a tall jug filled with fresh water inside a fancy bowl with a plug in the bottom to drain the dirty water off into the second jug mounted under the tabletop. A single chair was tucked up against the facing wall with a row of metal hooks hammered into the adobe above it.

Up in a corner of the room a spider was waiting for him to settle down so that it could get on with the web it was spinning.

There was a kerosene lantern mounted into a niche cut against the wall above the bed.

The room was cool and the bed was tempting. He tugged the buckle of his gunbelt loose and hung it over the bedhead. Then he placed the Bowie knife under his pillow and took off his shirt. He stripped, settling the throwing knife alongside the Bowie, and climbed under the sheets.

They were clean and cool and fresh-smelling. He closed his eyes and went to sleep in seconds.

The sound that woke him was indistinct as the presence of the wolf on the trail. His subconscious mind heard it and alerted him to potential danger, so that he rolled clear of the bed with the Colt in his right hand and the Bowie knife in his left, kicking the tangled sheet clear of his legs as he hit the floor on the far side of the bed.

Someone was knocking on the door.

He stood up, naked, the muzzle of the pistol held steady on the heavy panels. He paced silently round to fetch up against the wall. Sidled down until he was in a position to fire through the woodwork, then called out.

'Yeah? Who is it?'

'Linda, *señor* Gunn. Your bath is ready. You have been sleeping for more than four hours now.'

'Wait.' He backed away from the door and slid into his pants.

Still holding the Colt cocked and ready he paced over to the left-hand side and tripped the bolt.

'All right,' he called. 'Come on in.'

The door opened and the old man he had seen sweeping the foyer staggered in with a zinc tub cradled over his shoulders like the shell of some metallic tortoise. He set the thing down with a gusty sigh and scurried fast out of the room to make way for three Mexicans hefting buckets of steaming water that they tipped into the bath. The Mexicans left and Linda Velazquez came in. She was changed out of her green dress into something flowing and black and flimsy. She carried a big bar of soap in her right hand and a battered brush in her left. And an even bigger smile on her face.

She ushered in two more servants who set large buckets down on the floor then backed out of the room with down-turned faces and hidden smiles.

Then she kicked the door closed and slid the bolt.

'Your bath is ready,' she said softly. 'Why don't you get in?'

Azul looked at her. The room was dimly lit, but sufficient light filtered through the shutters to outline her body through the scanty confines of her robe. It was, at best, a thing solid as a cobweb, leaving the contours beneath barely hidden or careless to view.

He smiled and set the Colt down on the bed.

'Sure,' he said. 'Why not?'

He pulled his pants clear of his legs and stood up. Linda Velazquez ran a darting tongue over her lips. Her breath got faster and she reached up to unfasten the peignor from her body. Azul picked up his pistol and climbed into the bath. He set the weapon down alongside the tub, where he could reach it fast. His eyes were fixed on the woman.

The robe dropped to the floor. Under it she wore only a satin girdle that ended high above her thighs, straps of the same material connecting to the dark stockings couching her legs, between them the dark vee of her hair. At the top the girdle lifted her breasts, pushing them out so that the nipples stood dark and stiff and heavy above the smooth softness of the whaleboned silk.

Azul stretched back in the tub, admiring.

Slowly, enjoying his gaze, the woman tugged her suspenders loose of the stockings; slid each one slowly down her legs. She threw them carelessly on to the bed, then settled back to unfasten the girdle.

Naked, she was magnificent, a brown and copper goddess stepping slowly, enticingly, towards him.

She smiled and stooped down to lift the soap and the brush.

'*Pistolero*,' she murmured, 'I hope you live up to your reputation with weapons.'

Azul grinned. Reached out to grab her and tumble her over and down into the tub so that she splashed water, laughing, as she toppled across him.

'Scrub it,' he said. 'I feel dirty.'

CHAPTER TWO

The woman laughed.

It was a high-pitched, giggling sound with more fear in it than there was humour. It was the kind of sound a whore makes when she is uncertain of the temper of her client, when she doesn't quite know which way he might jump: to pay her over the odds; or mash her face into pulp.

Margie Robbins covered it with a fast move towards the whisky bottle standing up straighter than her customer on the dresser set against the far wall of her room. She got her hand steady enough to lift the bottle and tilt the neck down into the glasses set alongside. Her back hurt where he had hit her, and her trembling hand spilled liquor over the glass top of her *armoire*, spreading a faint amber pool across the protective glass. Nervously, she carried the two glasses back to the bed, sipping hers before she offered them to the man sprawled under the stained and sweaty sheets.

When he sat up and grabbed the glass she backed off, sipping the whisky to nurse feeling back into her body.

She crouched at the far end of the big bed, ogling the man lying mean and lazy at the head and wondering why she still found him so attractive.

It was hard to say exactly why: Margie had been a whore for the last seven years of her life, ever since her mother put her on the game when she was fourteen. Now she was twenty-one – looking over thirty – with a case of itchy chancre and bags under her baby-blue eyes to match the premature lines decorating her face.

Most of those could be hidden by powder; and the chancre was an occupational hazard that passing cowboys should know enough to avoid; or learn to live with.

But this new man was something else.

He walked into the Tucson Queen like he owned the place. And when he opened out his black coat and put the bills on the bar it looked like he did; or could, at the very least, buy it. The bankroll was that thick. He had swallowed a bottle of the good whisky fast and hungry before turning away from the long trestle to study the meat spread out through the saloon.

Margie had been settled down on a cowhand's knees just then. He was a nice, good-looking boy from off the HC spread; one of big John Cannon's boys, just in from the fall branding with money in his pockets and lust in his heart; or wherever – the exact placing didn't matter that much to Margie, not so long as it was there to be taken.

Then the man in the black coat just walked over and hauled her clear of Jim-Boy's knees, spinning her round like a top on the far end of his left arm so that she swung out and round and banged her blonde curls against the woodwork of the stairway.

Jim-Boy stood up of course and asked the man what in the goddam hell he thought he was playing at. Then the man in the dusty black jacket told Jim-Boy to shut his mouth and stay alive; because otherwise he would kill him stone dead. Which meant that Jim-Boy had to argue and reach for his gun, which was a Colt's Dragoon and very heavy. Not at all like the Frontier model Colt the man in the black suit hauled out and shot him with. Though *Hauled Out* wasn't exactly right, because the pistol had seemed to jump into his hand from under his jacket, and the smoke and flame had billowed long before Jim-Boy got his own pistol even part-way out.

The first shot had caught Jim-Boy high up in his chest, tipping him back over his chair so that his legs waved around looking silly while the second one blew away his handsome face.

His best friend, Buck, had pulled a gun then. And the

man in the black suit just swung his pistol round and squeezed the trigger. The bullet went into Buck's head just above his eyes, and exactly between them, so that he looked like one of those Greek monsters she had read about, a Cyclops or something. It hadn't lasted long because the blood just spurted out and covered up Buck's face like a red blanket. Then he fell down.

After that the man had just put his gun back in the holster and smiled at her. It wasn't a pleasant smile, but when he grabbed her arm again she hadn't resisted. She had told him about the chancre but that didn't seem to bother him: he just laughed and said he'd bigger things to worry about.

She had been with him for five days and wished that she had something worse. Like syphilis or smallpox. Something that could be passed with the maximum of suffering.

The first night hadn't been too bad. He had demanded no more than the usual services; which Margie could administer whilst almost asleep.

After that it had got worse. Day time he slept, or drank. In between trips to the stage depot and telegraph office, refusing to tell her why or what for. And when he drank he chose a table pulled up close to the windows, where he could see the street and anyone on it.

He seemed to be waiting for someone, though whether it was a friend or a man he planned to kill, he never told her. Margie doubted it would be a friend: he wasn't the kind of man who had many.

His name was Nolan. That was all she knew: he never had offered any other name and Margie was too nervous of him to ask.

He had been with her every night, using her with silent ruthlessness, like a machine that he employed out of habit, without feeling or care. Margie was long accustomed to casual encounters and didn't really expect any great show of affection. After all, business was business and she was in it for the money, not for love. But even so, most of her clients attempted some display of gallantry, a natural respect of women – or the appreciation of a rarely enjoyed commodity – prompting them to treat her almost like a lady. Not the way they would treat a decent married woman, or even a single girl, but at least like a person. Nolan didn't bother with any of that. He simply used her, and when she complained he beat her and reminded her that he had given her fifty dollars, with more to come; which was about as much as she might hope to make in a good month. It was the only reason she stuck with him.

That and the fact that she hoped to empty his bankroll one night and skip town.

The thought cheered her somewhat and she got to wondering if tonight might not be the right time. Nolan had been drinking steadily all day. The liquor didn't appear to have much effect on him, other than to dull his desire, which meant he took his pleasure in other ways. Margie had done her best to arouse him, utilising every trick she had learned during the long years between St Louis and Tucson, and a few she had made up herself. None had worked, so Nolan got mad and used his belt on her back. Margie had stuffed a wad of dirty sheet between her teeth and stifled her screams. Tears ran down her face, but her eyes stayed bright and full of hate.

After, when the rage was spent and her back was blue with bruises, Nolan had sent her downstairs for more whisky. One bottle was already three quarters empty.

Maybe, thought Margie, it could be tonight.

She rose from the bed, wincing as the skin across her spine and ribs stretched and burned, and brought the bottle over to the bed.

'More whisky, honey?'

She made her voice soft, as enticing as she knew how.

Nolan grunted and held out his glass. Margie topped it, added a splash to her own.

'What's the matter, honey? You act like you got big trouble.'

'Shut yore fuckin' mouth, whore.' Nolan drained his glass and held it out again. Margie emptied the first bottle. 'I'm thinkin'. I got problems you wouldn't understand.'

'Want to tell me?' Margie simpered, smiling through her pain. 'Might be better to share 'em. My momma always said that a trouble shared is a trouble halved.'

'Yore mother was a fuckin' whore, same as you.' Nolan's voice was flat, cold, only slightly slurred by the drink. 'Her mind was about as rotted as yours. Only trouble she ever knew was where to turn her next trick.'

Margie opened her mouth, ready to defend her mother's reputation. There wasn't very much to defend it with, because Annabelle Robbins had never had much of a reputation anyway, at least not amongst decent folk. Unless being the town lay was a reputation. Margie had a dim memory of a father with tired eyes and dirty hands, a beaten man who cried when the City Elders came round one night and told him to control his wife or leave St Louis. Annabelle hadn't been up to the standards demanded by the rich folks' brothels, so she turned her tricks in haylofts and back alleys; anywhere she could make the odd dollar for a stand-up or a go-down. Margie could still remember that night, even though she was half asleep and only nine years' old. Her momma had come home with hollow eyes and a torn dress, smelling of sweat and something else. Margie had watched through the crack of her bedroom door while her momma undressed and argued with her father. She remembered being surprised that momma had nothing on under her faded scarlet dress, and amazed when her poppa stood up and slammed a fist into momma's face. After that it all got hazy. Poppa wasn't there in the morning and for the next few weeks momma had a lot of friends – mostly men – coming by. They made a lot of noise that Margie could hear clearly through the flimsy walls of the shack, mostly groans and shouts. Some nights she couldn't sleep at all for the noise.

Then the Elders came back, this time with a constable. A few of the Elders looked embarrassed, and Margie thought she recognised their faces from earlier visits. In the morning momma had packed their clothes and a few other things and hitched up the mule to a broken-down wagon.

Some time later they got to Sedalia, where they stayed for several months. After that Margie's life had been one long journey. From Sedalia they drove west to Kansas City, then north to Fort Leavenworth, up to Council Bluffs and then west again to Fort Kearney and Julesburg. Margie rode her first train then, from Julesburg to Cheyenne. Then another, south to Denver. Momma was looking old by that time, and spent a lot of money on ointments that never quite stopped the sores from spreading over her body. They moved around a great deal for the next few years. Southwards to Colorado Springs, on to Pueblo, Trinidad, Taos, Santa Fe, Albuquerque, El Paso.

Annabelle Robbins died in Texas. By then she was blind and couldn't speak clearly because the roof of her mouth was rotted out. She lived on soup and whisky, provided by her fourteen years' old daughter.

By the time Margie celebrated her fifteenth birthday – in bed with a bald, fifty-years' old muleskinner – she knew all of her mother's tricks. She washed her mouth out with whisky morning and night-time, and bathed the other orifices of her body with neat liquor. When Annabelle finally croaked out her last, stale breath Margie left her in the cabin they had rented and bought herself a one-way ticket west on the Southern Pacific. She got off the train at Fort Yuma and spent the next five years catering to the needs of the soldiers and cowboys and traders who gathered around the confluence of the Gila and the Colorado.

Then she heard that Arizona was getting opened up by cattlemen with money to spend. She bought a ticket east and rode the black iron horse back to Tucson. The town looked good: she wasn't known there. She climbed down from the train and walked into town with a suitcase in her hand and a bright smile on her face. She was twenty years old and still better-looking than most of her professional sisters. She spent three hours walking the streets, checking out the saloons and whorehouses. The Tucson Queen looked to be the most prosperous so she went inside and offered her services to the owner. Jamey King tried her out himself and proclaimed her as tricksy a whore as any he'd tasted.

She was set up.

Now she was twenty-one and worried about her looks. She had six hundred dollars carefully banked, a slight scar on her left cheek where a drunken cowhand had slapped her while his spur was still in his hand, and a deep-seated hatred of just about everyone.

Though the hate was now mostly centred on Nolan.

'Don't you like me?' she asked. 'I been good to you, ain't I?'

'I pay for it,' snarled Nolan. 'You made more outta me than a dumb whore could make in weeks.'

'Be nice, honey,' she wheedled. 'Why not be nice? I been nice to you, ain't I? I keep you happy, don't I?'

'Shut up.' Nolan slumped back against the dirty pillows. 'Whores fuck, not talk.'

'You want another drink?' Margie used her teeth to pull the cork on the second bottle. The front two ached where Nolan had back-handed her. 'Why don't you take another slug an' then I'll see if I can't work you up a bit.'

She ran a tongue around her lips as she said it. Slowly, with her lashes fluttering in what she hoped was a lascivious invitation.

'Why not?' grunted Nolan. 'I paid enough for you.'

Margie smiled and filled his glass again. Then she slid off the bed to kneel alongside. Nolan eased back, shifting over to where she could reach him. He sipped his whisky slowly, eyes closed. Margie eased herself up so that her face was poised above his groin. She glanced at him – saw that he was waiting – and swiftly checked the bedhead. His gunbelt was looped over the far corner, the safety thong on the hammer of the Colt. The shoulder holster he wore under his black jacket was on the table; empty. The .38 Remington Star he carried in the hideaway was under the pillow, like the Colt, on the far side.

Margie lifted up, spreading her arms on either side of his waist. She eased her legs forward so that her weight rested on her knees and her right arm. Her left slid unobtrusively across the bed, towards the pillow. She ducked her head, teasing his member with puckered lips. Nolan grunted and dropped his empty glass. Margie smiled and opened her mouth, taking him in. She moved slowly, her head gliding down, then up, then down again. Her left hand crept over to touch the Remington.

Nolan tensed, thrusting his hips upwards against her face. Margie moaned in feigned ecstasy – they always liked that – and rested her fingertips against the butt of the pistol.

'You like that, honey?' She made her voice throaty, gasping. 'I sure do.'

'Eat, don't talk,' grunted Nolan.

Margie bobbed her head, setting to work with professional expertise. Nolan's eyes were closed and he lay back with his arms cradling his head. She teased him up, making a mental note to swill her mouth with alcohol when she was done.

Her fingers eased out, shoving the Remington deep under the pillow. She felt the barrel touch the wall as Nolan began to hump against her mouth and an involuntary gasp escaped his lips. Margie withdrew her hand. Her head moved faster and she essayed another throaty groan.

Maybe this would be the night . . .

Nolan grunted and she felt his hands fasten in her hair, shoving her down against his body. She kept on working. At least he bathed – was cleaner than most of her 'friends'.

Then his body tensed and his hands fell away. She opened her eyes and saw that he clutched the sheets. His hips arced upwards and he stared down at her shifting curls, his lips parted in what might have been a smile. Margie worked harder, using lips and tongue and teeth until he moaned and she felt her throat filled, a great deep shudder trembling through his body.

She swallowed and sat back, wiping a hand over her lips.

'How was that, baby? Was it good? You enjoy that?'

Nolan grunted.

'Fetch me a drink, whore.'

'Sure, honey. Rightaway.'

Margie stood up and filled both glasses. She handed one to Nolan and used the second to sluice her mouth. Hell! Face pox was something she could live without. She spat into the washstand, swilling the whisky around her tongue and gums. It burned where the teeth were loose, but the precaution was worthwhile.

She filled the glasses again and took a long swallow. Nolan emptied his in one. Margie tilted the bottle again. Nolan took longer drinking it, but the combined effects of sex and whisky were taking toll. He slumped back, yawning. Margie filled his glass.

He emptied it and fell back. Margie sipped her drink slowly, cautiously; waiting.

Nolan began to snore. He rolled on to his side, thrusting one hand under his pillow. Margie drew courage from the whisky. She emptied her glass and set it down gently on the table. Then she moved round to the far side of the bed. She eased the safety thong clear of the Colt's hammer and pulled the gun out from the holster. She tripped the loading gate back and thumbed the ejector spring to discharge the cartridges. She did it slowly, taking care to catch the unspent loads in her right hand. When the revolver was empty she put it back in the holster and dropped the shells into a drawer of the *armoire.*

Nolan's things were locked inside the wardrobe, the key in the pocket of his vest, hung on the wall. Margie found the key and opened the cupboard. It squeaked. She paused, holding her breath as fear threatened to spill her bowels over the faded carpet. Nolan snored and rolled over. Even from across the room, Margie could smell the whisky on his breath. She stood silent, not daring to move until a second rasping sound broke the silence.

Then she bent and opened the two saddlebags.

They were padded out, the contents bulking the leather so that the fastening straps were set on the last holes. She opened them.

And almost shrieked at what she saw.

The bags were thick with money.

Wads of ten and twenty dollar notes spilled out alongside singles and fifties. Greenbacks with pictures of Lincoln and Davies smiled up at her like old friends promising a better life. Margie's arithmetic was soundly based on the counting of notes and she knew that she was holding a fortune in her hands. She stuffed the bills back inside the saddlebags and buckled the straps down. For a moment she thought about getting dressed, then decided that gift horses don't wait and swung the bags over her shoulder.

Naked, she opened the door and ran down the corridor. A light showed under Marylou's door, so she knocked and called a soft greeting.

A man grunted irritably and Marylou shouted for whoever it was to go away.

Margie knocked again.

The door opened and Marylou stared bleary into the dim-lit corridor. Margie pushed inside before her friend had a chance to block the door, ignoring the naked man sitting up and staring from the bed.

'Gimme a dress,' she said, pushing Marylou towards the clothes cupboard. 'I'll pay you fifty dollars.'

'Christ, honey, what's the matter?' Marylou tugged her faded robe about her faded body. 'You in trouble?'

'No.' Margie fumbled a fifty-note clear of the saddlebag, using her body to hide the contents. 'I'm in luck, but I need a dress. Fast.'

She shoved the bill into Marylou's hand and stood up. The cowboy stared at her.

'Christ!' he said. 'We goin' a double?'

Margie ignored him. She followed Marylou over to the wardrobe and hauled a demure black dress clear of the rail. She tugged it on and picked up a pair of side-button boots. Then, almost an afterthought, a suspender belt and stockings. Oblivious of the ogling cowboy, she hiked up the dress and clipped the belt around her waist, rolled the stockings up her legs and fastened them in place. Then she put the boots on and stood up.

'You got a coat?'

'You leavin'?'

'You bet. I'll pay you fifty fer a decent coat.'

Marylou shoved her aside and reached back to the left, delving deep into the space behind her dresses. She came out with a dark blue calico coat.

Margie fumbled a second fifty out of the saddlebags and climbed into the coat. It fitted badly, tight across her breasts and shorter than she liked around the ankles, but as good as she could hope to get. She left it open as she ran from the room.

Then she halted and turned back, tugging a note out. It was a hundred dollar bill.

'Listen,' she said as Marylou grabbed it, 'you ain't seen me. You ain't seen me since I went upstairs with Nolan. You never sold me no dress an' you don't know where I am.'

'Right, honey,' said Marylou. 'I can't even remember yore name.'

'Oh Christ!' moaned the cowboy. 'We gonna fuck or talk?'

Margie walked out of the Tucson Palace feeling like a

lady for the first time in her life. She headed straight for the SP depot and bought herself a ticket to Yuma. It was four in the morning and the train wasn't due in until six. She hoped Nolan would stay asleep that long.

Otherwise, she knew, she'd be dead.

Nolan woke up with his mouth tasting like a stable floor and a dull throbbing behind his eyes. He felt hung-over and mean, but a sense of unease overrode the effects of the alcohol. There was something wrong. He knew that even before he forced his gummy lids open and saw that the other side of the bed was empty. Automatically, he reached under the pillow for the Remington. The pistol was moved and when he groped for it, he succeeded only in pushing it clear of the mattress. The clatter it made hitting the boards lanced pain through his aching skull and he cursed noisily, shouting for Margie.

There was no answer and he rolled across the bed, hauling the Colt from the holster. The weight was all wrong and he realised that the gun was emptied. He dropped it on the sheets as he sprang over to the cupboard.

Then gasped and swore again when he saw the saddle-bags were gone. Desperately, he fumbled in the rear of the closet. His fingers closed on a flat, oilskin-wrapped package. Nolan tugged it out and pulled the string loose: the package held two metal plates, printing plates, front and back for a five dollar bill.

A slow sigh of relief escaped his thinned-out lips, swiftly replaced by a grunt of pure fury. He fastened the package and thrust it to the back of the closet. Then he grabbed the Remington off the floor and loaded the Colt. He dressed hastily, his mind working fast and furious.

The goddam thieving bitch whore had lifted his money, which meant she was running. But to where? Tucson wasn't big enough to hide her, so the chances were that she'd try to quit town as fast as she could. He glanced out at the pre-dawn mist. It was about five, close to sun-up. There wouldn't be a stage through until noon, but there was an early train – his best bet. He locked the room and went down the stairs at a run.

Tucson was brightening up as the sun rose, but the street was empty. The fancy clock built into the frontage of the bank across the way struck the half hour. Nolan took off at a run, heading for the station. Raw anger gripped him, almost overcoming the sense of caution he knew he must adopt. He couldn't afford to let people see the contents of the saddlebags, that would lead to too many questions, all of them pointing back to the bank the money had come from. His anger mounted as he realised how close Margie was to blowing his carefully-made plans wide open. He had already invested close on a month and better than one thousand dollars setting up a deal with a crooked printer. It had taken time to locate the man and arrange for him to come north out of Mexico to the nearest town large enough to furnish the equipment they would need to use the plates. He was due to arrive in Tucson any time now, and they would need the ready cash to get the operation started. The ready cash and a minimum of fuss.

A stray dog snapped at Nolan as he ran by. The dark man kicked the animal yelping across the street.

The sun came through the mist and outlined the Southern Pacific depot. Nolan paused, staring at the squat building. The rails went past Tucson on the north side, so the depot was built slightly apart from the main body of the town. It consisted of a sprawl of cattle pens and a solitary, single-storey cabin housing the ticket office and a little waiting room. There was a low wooden platform fronting the building and a curl of woodsmoke drifting from the chimney. On the platform he could see a figure in a dark coat pacing nervously up and down the planking.

Off to the east, mournful and shrill in the silent morning, he heard a train whistle blow.

He broke into a run.

Margie saw him coming and shrieked.

Abe Zachary looked up from his coffee and glanced at the gold hunter on the desk before him. Fifteen minutes ahead of schedule. Merle must have piled on the steam to make up that amount of time. Maybe he was trying to break his own record, or maybe he was anxious to see that fancy woman he had shacked up in Los Angeles. The thought reminded Abe of the lone passenger waiting outside. Funny thing that, ole Margie jumping town in so almighty a hurry. Abe chuckled: might be she'd got her marching orders, or maybe it was just the whores' wanderlust. Funny, though, that she only had two saddlebags with her; women usually travelled with a pile of cases and doo-dads.

He blew his nose and slid the ticket window open, shoving his head out to call Margie's attention.

Only Margie wasn't there anymore. Abe shook his head and pushed through the door into the waiting room. She wasn't there, either. He snorted, grumbling at the vagaries of women in general, and went out on to the platform.

Margie was fifty feet down the track, running towards the approaching engine. She had her skirts hiked up around her thighs and looked like the devil himself was coming after her. Considering the fact that she wore high heels and was dragging the saddlebags behind her, she was making good time. Why she was running, Abe couldn't figure: the train was stopping anyway, and she wouldn't halt it any faster by going to meet it.

Then something slammed into Abe's back and he pitched headlong on to the platform. He cursed and looked up in time to see a tall man dressed all in black go charging down the rails after the fleeing woman. He sat up, rubbing his chin and wondered what in the hell was going on.

The train hooted again, slowing as it approached the depot.

Margie kept on running, not daring to look back.

Nolan paced his strides to land on the sleepers, gaining ground fast.

There was a third shrill whistle, this time a warning.

Margie stumbled, a heel hooking on a loose pin. She almost fell, fighting to regain her balance without dropping the money-filled saddlebags.

And Nolan reached her.

He grabbed her shoulder and hauled back. Margie screamed. She dropped the bags and lurched forwards, sliding her arms clear of Marylou's coat. The move took Nolan by surprise and he stumbled back with the calico garment flapping in his hand. Margie picked up the bags and began to run again, straight at the approaching engine.

Nolan cursed and threw the coat aside. He lunged forwards and got a hand on the neck of Margie's dress. The flimsy material ripped, tearing away from her back so that it spilled free of her shoulders and tangled her arms. One breast flopped heavily into view.

Fear and greed overcame her initial panic and she swung round, grasping the saddlebags in both hands. Nolan was reaching for her again, but the flailing blow caught him on the side of the face, knocking him across the rails. He snarled and lifted his left arm to fend off Margie's return swipe. He stepped inside the blow and rammed his clenched fist hard into her stomach. Margie gasped and doubled over. Nolan reached out to snatch the bags. The woman tried to fight him off, but he used his right hand to seize her exposed breast. He squeezed, digging his fingers deep into her flesh, twisting. Margie screamed. Nolan yanked the bags clear of her grip, the motion dragging her towards him.

She reached up raking her painted nails down his face. Four dark lines showed on Nolan's cheek, abruptly filling with blood that ran down his jaw and dripped on to his shirt. He jerked her head back. Margie stepped in and drove a knee at his groin. Nolan grunted, staggering back as nausea flooded his belly and he tasted bile thick in his mouth. Margie stooped for the saddlebags.

Nolan forced himself upright, rage clouding out the pain, and swung a fist against the woman's face.

Margie's head snapped back and her lower lip got bloody where her teeth bit into the flesh. She staggered, trying hard to hold on to the bags. Nolan stamped on her hand. She screamed as his boot crushed the delicate bones connecting her fingers to her wrist. Nolan kicked her in the stomach and she felt herself lifted up and back, the painful thud of the rail against her back.

'Goddam whore!' Nolan grabbed the saddlebags and tossed them clear of the rails. 'I'm gonna teach you, bitch!'

The whistle shrilled again and the eight wheels of the big Baldwin 4-4-0 screamed a metallic protest as the engineer dragged the brake all the way down. Sparks candled from the rails, filling the air with the smell of burning.

Nolan reached down to grab a fistful of hair. He yanked Margie up, then slammed her head back across the rail. Bright lights exploded across her vision and she barely felt the pain of Nolan's weight slamming down against her stomach. She was dimly aware of a roaring, shrieking sound, but couldn't be sure if it was her own voice, or Nolan's, or the approaching engine.

Dimly, she was aware of Abe running up the track with his arms waving in a futile attempt to halt the skidding train. She spat on Nolan's face and tried to claw him again, but her left hand was useless, the fingers limp, and her right was pinned to her side by the dark man's knees.

'Bastard' she moaned. 'They'll get you fer this.'

Nolan grinned and glanced to his right. The engine was close now, sliding onwards like a heavy metal avalanche. He leaned back, using his legs to hold the woman down.

At the last moment he threw himself clear, feeling sparks burn his face and hands.

Margie felt the weight go from her and raised her head. She saw the dusty prow of the cowcatcher looming above her, sunlight glinting bright on the forward lantern. A man was shouting, but she could barely hear the sound above the screaming of the locked wheels.

She realised what Nolan had done and opened her mouth to scream. But it was too late. Something hit her on the side of her head and the sun blinked out in a great red wash.

The cowcatcher pulped Margie Robbins's temple, snapping her neck so that her head twisted over and down under the grillwork. The big train went on sliding, tugging the body round under the wheels. Several tons of metal ran over Margie's corpse, grinding it like so much minced meat. One foot, severed from the leg, flew clear, bouncing in a spray of crimson across the sand. The engine ground to a halt halfway down the platform. The fuel wagon and one coach went over what was left of Margie. After that there wasn't much more to go over, just a long, red smear down the rails and a few tattered remnants of cheap cloth.

Abe Zachary bent over and vomited. Merle climbed down from the cab, wondering if he would be able to make up his time. The engineer stared wide-eyed at the rails. Nolan picked up the saddlebags and began to walk away.

A shout stopped him and he turned, hefting the bags over his left shoulder, his right hand dropping to the gun holstered on his waist.

He looked into the barrels of a Remington scattergun. Both hammers were cocked and the brakeman holding the big gun looked angry enough to use it.

'That was murder,' he said in a hoarse, shocked voice. 'Plain, cold-blooded murder.'

Nolan stared back. 'She stole somethin' from me,' he said. 'I was gettin' it back.'

'You killed her,' said the brakeman in the same horrified voice. 'I saw the whole thing. You killed her.' He turned to Merle. 'We'd best wait up. Someone better go fetch the sheriff so we can hand this feller over.'

'Ah, shit,' grumbled Merle. 'There goes my schedule.'

Nolan knew better than to argue with a cocked shotgun. He let them march him back to the depot while Abe ran to fetch the sheriff. The brakeman kept the shotgun pointed at him while they waited, his face pale with outrage and disgust.

'You're makin' a whole lotta fuss over nuthin',' grunted Nolan. 'She was only a cheap whore. All I did was put her back on the rails.'

CHAPTER THREE

Linda Velazquez stretched lazily across the big bed.

Autumn sunlight danced dust in languid spirals through the air, pooling shadow beneath the up-thrust of her breasts, along the smooth skin of her parted thighs. She sighed, taking pleasure in the memory of the night before. It had been a long time since she knew a man like this one, this one they called Breed. In a few days, she knew, he would be gone. But for now . . . Hai! *Maria Purisima! Que hombre!*

She rolled over, smelling the night's heady scent on the crumpled sheets, and waited for him to emerge from her private bathroom.

He was dressed when he came out, buckling his gunbelt around his waist and staring at her with those blue eyes that hid fire inside the clear gaze.

'Where are you going, *querido*?' she asked.

'To the saloon.' His voice was guttural, accenting his fluent Spanish with the overtones of his Apache childhood. 'There might be news come in.'

'And if not?' She was almost afraid to hear the question answered. 'What then?'

He shrugged. 'I'll head up to Tucson an' look round.'

'And then?'

He grinned, not bothering to reply. Instead, he picked up his hat and went out through the door, leaving the woman to sigh again and dream.

Two days, now, he had been in Tubac. Longer than planned, but nonetheless enjoyable. The *viuda* Velazquez would be happy to have him stay on indefinitely, that he knew, but he had no wish to become part-owner of a rooming house, despite the gains – physical and financial – that she offered him. If there was no word today, he decided, he would ride on come morning. Head north into Tucson and continue the hunt there. He felt rested and refreshed, eager to go on after Nolan for all the tempting blandishments of Linda Velazquez.

Out on the street the sun was blinding bright, getting lower in the sky as winter approached. He settled the flat-crowned Sonora stetson on his mane of blond hair and tilted the flat brim down to shade his eyes. Tubac looked sleepy and still, the lassitude of noonday extending even to the horses hitched along the street and the idly-scratching cur dogs, panting under the sidewalks.

He stepped down off the porch and walked over to the saloon.

The Royal Grand had a name far in excess of its modest pretensions. It sold watery Mexican beer, home-brewed whisky, and fierce tequila. For those customers seeking fast oblivion – and prepared to risk their stomach linings and their sight – it carried a stock of *pulque*. It was a flat-roofed structure of adobe and wood, with sawdust on the bare planking of the floor and a long trestle rested on empty barrels stretching down one wall. The windows were fly-blown and dusty, most of the interior light coming in through the bead-hung doorway. There were tables and chairs spread out through the low-ceilinged room, and a wood door at the far end that opened into a slant-roofed shack where the local whore held court. She was a forty years' old Mexican who doubled as cook and favoured a yellow corn-cob pipe when she wasn't working.

Azul went up to the bar and ordered whisky. He got a clay drinking pot and a bottle with no label. The cork was dented with teeth marks and the underside of the bottle had three crushed flies stuck to it. The whisky was sour and burning. He called for a beer.

The tepid liquid took away the bite of the spirit and he leaned back against the bar, studying the customers.

Three Mexicans were playing a desultory hand of poker at one *centavo* a time and four Americans were pulling faces at the bottles in front of them. They looked like cowhands, to judge by their faded denims and grubby shirts. Their guns were hiked back behind their hips so they didn't interfere with the cards, and their faces were tired and lost. There was a Mexican slumped against the far wall with his sombrero slanted down over his face and his legs stuck out in front of the table. He wore big silver spurs and had a half-empty bottle of *pulque* in his hand. Azul noticed that he wore a fancy gunbelt, all silver conchos and decorative filigree. The holster was loose from his hip, with the butt of a Colt's Peacemaker sticking up out of the tooled leather. The butt was notched three times.

Farther down into the shadows was a second Mexican with a fat face and a huge moustache. His sweat-stained shirt was draped with a double bandoleer and he wore a Smith & Wesson American butt-forwards under the down-spread of his belly. There was a Winchester propped against the wall on his left. It was clean and oiled and rested where he could reach it fast. He lifted a pitcher of tequila while Azul looked at him, wiping the residue of the liquor from his moustache with the back of his left hand.

Across from the fat Mexican, at a table set midway between the end of the bar and the whore's room, was a grey-suited American. He had a whisky bottle and a mug of beer to the left of the table. Azul noticed that he drank with his left hand; the right stayed flat on the table top, the fingers drumming against the wood. He wore a dusty three-piece suit, the colour matching the curly-brimmed derby on the table beside his twitching fingers.

Not one of them paid anything more than cursory attention to Azul, so he turned back to the bar and called the tender over.

'Well?' he asked. 'You see him?'

The man shook his head. 'Ain't been no strangers through since you come in. Leastways, not that I seen.'

'You hear anything from the cantina?' Azul sipped his drink. 'Any word round town?'

The barkeep shook his head again.

'Nuthin'. Them three got in this morning.' He ducked his head down the bar. 'The Mexes I figger fer *pistoleros* lookin' fer someplace quiet outside o' their own country. The yankee's a drummer, I guess. He ain't been nowhere 'cept here since he arrived. The greasers got a camp a mile outta town, they said. I reckon they don't have the money fer a decent room.'

Azul nodded his thanks and turned back to the bottle. A footfall brought his head round to stare at the fat Mexican. The man was on his feet, walking slowly over to the bar with the pitcher dangling in his left hand while he wiped his right over his spreading moustache. He dumped the pot on the trestle and smiled at Azul.

'Hot, isn't it?' He smiled lazily. 'A man gets bored with this kind of weather. Makes him mean.'

'Yeah,' said Azul. 'That's true.'

The man picked up his refilled flask and went back to his table. Azul turned back towards the bar. Then became aware of the second Mexican standing beside him. The sombrero was thrown back behind his neck and Azul realised that the big silver spurs were welded into place so that the rowels couldn't turn. He glanced down, wondering why he hadn't heard the man approach. What he had thought to be dust spread over the soles and heels of the fancy boots was grey felt, tacked on to the leather so that the Mexican could walk like a man barefooted on a soft carpet.

The Mexican smiled. He had big, even teeth, very clean. He was young – maybe twenty – and looked confident.

The Peacemaker was clear from the holster, dangling loose in the Mexican's hand. It hung close to his right hip, hidden from view between his body and Azul's. The hammer was cocked and his finger was tight on the trigger.

'I think that you are called Gunn,' he said softly. 'Matthew Gunn. You are also known as Azul. Or Breed. Whatever the name, there is a reward. In Fronteras they say you are worth five hundred dollars for the killing of Amos Grieve. It is not a great deal of money, but it is enough.'

'This ain't Fronteras,' said Azul. 'That place is a whole long ride from here.'

'It doesn't matter,' smiled the Mexican. 'A dead man gives no trouble on a journey.'

'You come a long way for five hundred,' murmured the half-breed. 'Pity you wasted all that time.'

He moved as he spoke, shifting his weight on to his right leg as his arm swept up and round to spill his whisky over the bounty hunter's face. At the same time his left hand went out like a striking diamond back, clasping tight around the gun, crushing the fingers over trigger and hammer. His left leg swept sideways, kicking the Mexican's right out from under him. The Colt exploded a bullet into the floor as the man yelped with the pain of the raw liquor burning his eyes.

Azul twisted, dragging the body down on to his left shoulder, turning to throw the man across his crouched form like a shield. He held on to the down-flung hand as he heard the sharp bark of a Winchester, and felt splinters blast from the bar. The man he was holding screamed. There was the dull *click* of the rifle's action.

Azul powered to his feet, pitching the Mexican out and forwards at the far wall.

The Winchester boomed. The man in the air screamed again as the bullet ripped through his body, shattering his left shoulder. He hit the floor and rolled over, groaning as he crawled towards his companion.

Azul dropped to the right, drawing his Colt as he fell.

A third rifle shot ploughed splinters from the woodwork behind him. He hit the floor and rolled, firing blind. The fat Mexican was on his feet, levering the rifle. Azul fired back. His bullet hit the man two inches below the bandoliers, just beneath the vee of his rib-cage. It tore through the soft spread of his belly, puncturing the stomach sac before blasting out through his spine. Shards of bone and crimson blood gouted after the bullet, leaving a great spray of crimson like spilled liquor over the planking. The Mexican grunted and staggered back. Azul shot him again. The second bullet ripped into his face, pulping the nose so that the moustache got suddenly red and began to drip over the fleshy lips.

The fat man sat down. The Winchester fell from his hands as he reached up to hold his shattered face. It was a reflex action: he was dead while he did it, only the automatic pressures of his wasted nerve-endings controlling his movements. Blood spilled from between his clutching fingers, then he fell back, prompting a gout of blood like a fountain from his holed stomach. His head made a loud thud against the boards.

The younger Mexican crawled over to the body. His broken arm dragged behind him and blood showed on his face where he had rammed into the floor. He reached out to haul the S & W clear of the dead man's holster, thumbing back the hammer as he pitched himself behind the overturned table, using that and the corpse for cover.

'Don't,' said Azul. 'You're wasting time.'

'Five hundred American.' The Mexican's voice was hoarse. 'That's enough.'

'Not to die for,' said Azul, squeezing the trigger.

Colt and S & W detonated at the same time. Azul was dropping back on to the floor as he fired; the Mexican had his pistol angled up. The .44 bullet spent itself somewhere behind the half-breed. The .45 took away the upper part of the *pistolero's* skull, dropping a great chunk of bloodied bone back into his sombrero.

The Mexican tilted back, arms spreading wide as the S & W dropped from nerveless fingers. Blood covered his face, spouting down over his shirt, covering the silverwork of his gunbelt, the conchos and stitching of his fancy pants. He opened his mouth, but only more blood came out and he pitched back with blank eyes staring at the spattered ceiling.

Azul climbed to his feet, thumbing fresh cartridges into the warm Colt.

'No strangers?' he said, turning back towards the bar.

He stopped when he saw the barkeep slumped under the trestle. The man was spread out in a wide pool of spreading blood that pulsed from his chest, where a neat, round hole showed red against his shirtfront.

'Messy, ain't it?' Azul spun round to face a grey-suited drummer. 'Killing mostly is.'

'You want some?' he asked, holding the Colt level on the man's chest. 'I'd as soon as walk out of here without shootin' you.'

'No need.' The man shook his head, holding his arms out away from his sides. 'All I want it is to make you a proposition.'

'So did they,' grunted Azul, glancing at the dead Mexicans.

'Bounty killers,' sneered the American. 'One hell of a way to make a livin'.'

'So what's yours?' grunted Azul.

'Detective. I'm with the Pinkerton Agency.'

He drew the left side of his jacket clear of his body, exposing a stubby revolver in a used-looking shoulder holster. Keeping his eyes tight on Azul's face, he pulled a leather wallet clear of the inside pocket, flipped it open. Azul stared at the metal badge. It was stamped with the emblem of an eye and the legend printed around the symbol read: The Eye That Never Sleeps.

'So?' grunted the half-breed. 'What's that to do with me?'

'A man called Nolan,' said the Pinkerton. 'I want to hire you to find him. There's five hundred dollars in it.'

Azul studied the badge. 'I guess,' he murmured, 'that the eye has the vote.'

CHAPTER FOUR

The Pinkerton was called Carmady. He was a heavy-set man with a face that looked like it had seen most of the sights on the underside of life and chosen to shrug them off. Shaved, he looked better, almost kindly.

He had manners, too, thanking Linda Velazquez as she served whisky in her private rooms; and a close mouth. The woman took the hint and left them alone, promising to send food in. She kissed Azul before leaving.

'Nice set-up,' commented the detective. 'Wish I could afford it.'

Azul ignored the crack.

'You want Nolan,' he said. 'How come you'll pay me to find him?'

Carmady shrugged: 'You know the country; I don't. I work mostly outta Texas: San Antonio, Houston . . . round there. Range Detective, that's my speciality. I never even heard o' this feller until we got word in from Washington.'

He sipped his drink, waiting for Azul to say something.

The half-breed looked at him from over the rim of the glass, waiting out the silence.

Carmady swallowed half his whisky and put the tumbler down.

'Word is that you know him. Been lookin' for him a long time.'

Azul nodded. 'Yeah. We got a personal score needs settling.'

'Don't give out much, do you?' said Carmady. 'The offer interest you, or not?'

'Killing Nolan,' said Azul, 'interests me. I'm not keen on handing him over to the law. Like I said: it's a personal thing.'

Carmady chuckled and pulled a sheet of paper from his jacket. He spread it out and began to read.

'The *Federales* in Galenas got a hundred an' fifty offer on you. The Texas Rangers is still puttin' up two hundred fer that sergeant you shot. There's a hundred dollars fer bustin' jail in Avila. An' I heard it said the Mexes would pay five hundred American to see you back in Fronteras.'

'I thought the Texan bill was cancelled,' said Azul; carefully.

'Not so,' grinned Carmady. 'You're worth close on a grand to the man who kills you.' He folded the paper and put it back inside his jacket. 'Makes you worth a whole lot more'n me.'

'It's nice to feel wanted,' rasped Azul. 'It sets a value on things. How come you aren't trying for it?'

'You're worth more alive,' grinned Carmady. 'If I can claim bounty on Nolan, I stand to make twice that.'

'So why ask me to help?' Azul wondered why he was beginning to like the man. 'Why not do it on your own?'

'Like I said,' Carmady filled his glass and pushed the bottle over to the half-breed, 'you know him. You'll know better'n me where he is, recognise him faster. Also, you ain't bound by the same rules as me. Bein' a

Pinkerton operative I gotta stay more or less inside the law.'

Azul grinned and topped his glass: 'Why the big hunt?'

'Three reasons,' said Carmady. 'Nolan lifted around seventy thousand off a bank robber called Amos Grieve. That's enough on its own to set up a big search, but he got two printin' plates as well. The kind that roll five dollars at a time.'

'Like coughin' up money,' murmured Azul.

Carmady didn't understand. He said: 'And he killed two of our men, as well. Harvey and Mitchell.'

'I heard,' said Azul. 'I was close when it happened.'

'Yeah,' said Carmady. 'I got word on that.'

Azul topped the glasses. 'So you want me to go lookin' for him? No holds barred an' five hundred dollars reward. Suppose I lift his plates? What then?'

'Be stupid,' said Carmady. 'Any kind of set-up like that leaves traces. We'd find you. You'd face twenty years in Leavenworth or Yuma. It'd be a fool's move.'

'Specially for a half-breed,' grunted Azul. 'What's Nolan face?'

'You,' said the Pinkerton. 'I got word from the top that the boss people'll work to scrub your record if you co-operate. This side o' the border, at least. That, an' the five hundred. You interested?'

Azul nodded: 'Yeah.'

'Good,' said Carmady. 'I'll pay you now.'

'Not after?' asked the half-breed. 'Not when you're sure I done the job?'

Carmady smiled. 'Why? I'll take yore word. An' if you don't keep it I can always find you again.'

Azul smiled back and took the money. They shook hands on the deal as one of Linda's girls came in with food. There was a mess of enchilladas piled up on a big platter, steaming and giving off a rich, tangy odour of spiced meat. A pitcher of beer, packed inside a bowl of ice accompanied the food. A second girl brought in a bottle of French wine, then the first appeared again with huge steaks and a platter of greens. Hash brownies were served and then – a luxury – a bowl of canned peas. Afterwards, coffee and a decanter of brandy.

'Christ!' Carmady sat back and wiped a hand over his mouth. 'I ain't eaten that good since I left home.'

'What happens when I find Nolan?' asked the half-breed. 'What proof will you want that I've killed him?'

'Guess yore word's enough,' said Carmady. 'Anyways, I'll hear about it. Best thing, I guess, is fer me to stick around here, so you'll know where to find me. If you head up to Tucson it ain't gonna be too difficult to contact me.'

'Why Tucson?' asked Azul. 'Why not El Paso or Tombstone? Maybe Yuma?'

Carmady grinned. 'Hell! If he'd gone to El Paso I'd've heard by now. Tombstone ain't nuthin' more'n a cow-town – a spread o' saloons an' cathouses. Yuma's too full o' law to be worthwhile. Nolan has to be lookin' fer a wide open town with money in it an' no questions. Also, he's gonna need machinery to print with. Tucson's the obvious place. Were I as knowledgeable about the man as you, I'd head straight up there.'

'So why don't you?'

'Like I said: you know him better'n me. You got a better chance o' findin' him. An' I have to steer clear o' the law a certain amount.'

The argument held a certain degree of weight. Not quite enough to convince Azul, but sufficient – allied to his desire to find and kill Nolan – to swing it in his favour. There were reasons enough to doubt that Carmady was telling him the whole truth, but the five hundred notes were a heavy weight in favour of going through with the deal.

He emptied his glass and went to find Linda Velazquez.

She was sorry to see him go, but accepted the inevitability of his departure with dry eyes and a smile that said she hoped to see him come back. As he walked away from the rooming house, he noticed that she was looking at Carmady with a speculative glaze in her wide, dark eyes.

He got the black horse out of the stable and rode away into the afternoon, a lonely figure in an empty country. Tucson was around seventy-five miles to the north, a long swing up the course of the Santa Cruz river with nothing between except dry sand and cactus. It was a wide open landscape, the kind he was accustomed to, and loved, the kind his Apache kinfolk roamed. It would take him, he knew, two days – perhaps longer – to cross. But then there would be Tucson, and the promise of vengeance.

He heeled the big black pony to a fast canter over the wastelands, anxious to settle the long-held score with destiny. And the dark man called Nolan.

Nolan was fractionally more comfortable, but enjoyed considerably less freedom.

He sat inside a cell in the Tucson jail, on a bare pine bench held against the wall by two rusty brackets and a pair of rusty chains. Across the cell was a bunk, propped against the wall on two columns of rough-cut adobe bricks. The bunk was covered with a thin mattress of cheap cotton stuffed with straw. There was a pillow of the same coarse material and a rough wool blanket spread over the bunk. Bugs scurried busily across the wool. Between the bunk and the bench was a narrow window, the afternoon sunlight bisected by the steel bars set into the stone of sill and frame.

The third wall of the cell was comprised of nine feet high metal rods. They went down deep into the stone floor, and were set into the adobe roof with wide steel plates bolted into the wet concrete and left to dry there before the cell was used. The roof was adobe reinforced with matting and branches.

There was a door-cage hung into the frontal bars of the cell. It rested on three solid steel hinges, fastening on a big, metal-plated lock that had only one key hole. On the outside.

Nolan had been there for three days.

There was nothing inside the cell, apart from the bunk and the bench and a can of water. And a big, fat spider spinning a web across the roof. The web was thick with flies and other insects. It looked like it had been a long time in the making. The spider's movements were the only entertainment Nolan got.

The cell was at the far end of the jail, separated from the other cages by a narrowing of the adobe walls, so that the dark man couldn't even see his fellow prisoners. There didn't anyway, appear to be too many other inmates. Just a sprinkling of drunks and the odd pick-pocket. Nolan had his saddlebags with him and knew that his other gear was held in the sheriff's office out front. Big George Gilman was an honest lawman. Hard, but honest. Nolan believed him when he said he hadn't gone through the gear collected out of the saloon.

Gilman was holding him until word came from Yuma.

Abe Zachary, Merle Haggard – the driver of the train – and the brakeman, Martin Parton, had all testified to his killing. That was enough for Gilman to hold him in custody. Margie Robbins had been murdered, that was clear. Not only according to Abe, Haggard and Parton, but also according to the early-rising passengers looking out the windows of the Dawn Flyer at the man shoving the whore under the wheels.

It wasn't as if Margie was worth too much trouble, but with that many witnesses, Gilman didn't have over-much choice. He had to take Nolan in and hold him until he got official word back from the high-hats in Yuma.

The sooner it came, the better. The man made Gilman nervous, and the sheriff looked forward to seeing him off. One way or another. It was not unlikely that Nolan belonged to a gang, and Gilman had taken the precaution of putting his deputies on double shifts. There were three, all solid, reliable men, if somewhat dis-gruntled at the extra duty. Gilman worked it that one stayed on guard in the office at all times and organised a new timetable of rounds that allowed the lawmen to walk out in pairs. The town was pretty quiet now that the Fall branding was done and the cowhands' week-long spree gotten over. There was always the odd drunk to contend with, and the occasional fight, but nothing that Gilman couldn't handle.

Except Nolan. There was an air of pure evil about the man that set Gilman to worrying for no obvious reason, and since the cell door closed behind him Gilman had had the feeling that a big black cloud hung over Tucson.

It was like waiting for a duststorm. When the air gets very still and you suddenly realise that something is coming without being quite sure what it is. Except that you sense it's dangerous.

Gilman had met his share of killers. In Lordsburg he had once gone up against an aspiring gunslinger armed with a cut-down scattergun: Billy Antrill was one of the three men he had shot dead. In Pecos he had killed John Fremont when the outlaw tried to rob the stage depot. And in Prescott he had faced two brothers who shot a barkeep because they didn't like the taste of his whisky. Zeke Holden had died with the first bullet; Abner had been carried away with his gun hand shattered. Gilman was a good lawman who knew how to take care of himself. He wasn't given to imaginings, and so felt doubly uneasy about the feeling Nolan brought on.

He believed in the law and its proper, democratic, observance. That was why he was holding the green-eyed whore killer until he got word out of Yuma. Tucson didn't have its own judge yet, so major offenders were shipped up the line to be tried by due process of the established court with its resident judge. It would have been easier back in Lordsburg or Pecos: the mayor or the City Elders could have convened a court, appointed a jury, found Nolan guilty and hung him. Nice, tight, and all legal. In a larger township there would have been a regular court to settle the matter fast, taking it all out of Gilman's hands.

In Tucson all he could do was wait.

He had taken sworn depositions from Abe and Merle and Martin, plus a list of those train passengers who had witnessed the murder. A report had been sent to Yuma with the delayed train. Now it was only a question of waiting. And hoping the ominous feeling of impending danger was misplaced.

Gilman was making his nightly rounds in company with Lyle Watson when he saw the stranger ride in.

Lyle was over on the far side of mainstreet checking doors like Gilman as they worked their way up from the eastern end towards the central hub of saloons and whorehouses. Both lawmen carried scatterguns canted across their left arms. The big Meteors were cut down to about eighteen inches apiece and loaded with savage ought-ought shot, the kind that will pick a man up and blow his body apart at fifteen feet; or send a crowd running for fear of the spreading pattern of heavy-gauge pellets.

Lyle saw the stranger first and whistled to attract Gilman's attention. The big lawman ducked inside a doorway and had the shotgun's hammers thumbed back, the muzzles angling streetwards, before he even knew someone was coming.

Lyle faded off into the shadows, only the double *click* of his own weapon revealing his position.

The rider came in slow and easy. A lighted window outlined him briefly as he came out on to mainstreet and Gilman saw a man slumped in the saddle with the weary set of a long ride disguising the lean ranginess of his body. He wore a dark hat with blond hair spilling out from under the brim, and faded clothes, stained with dust. His horse looked tired, the black head drooping down like it was anxious to sleep and eat. The man looked like any other saddlebum, except for the knee-high Apache moccasins and the gunbelt.

Gilman noticed the belt first. It was clean and oiled, the holster canted round on to the left hip. There was a Bowie sticking up out of a plain leather sheath, hilt forwards on the right side. And the man's right hand stayed close to the pistol.

He glanced up as he came out on to mainstreet and Gilman wondered how he knew he was being watched.

The lawman stepped out to where the rider could see him.

'Welcome to Tucson!' He kept the Meteor levelled on the man's belly. 'Guess you're new in town.'

'Yeah. I am.'

The rider ducked his head in greeting, then turned towards Lyle.

'You always meet visitors with scatterguns?'

He lifted his hand away from the Colt, resting it on his saddlehorn.

'You got good eyes, stranger.' Gilman eased the hammers down, sensing the moment of danger was passed. 'What brings you here?'

Azul smiled briefly. 'Business,' he said.

'What kind?'

Gilman stepped out on to the sidewalk so that light glanced off the brass star pinned to his jacket.

'Personal,' said Azul.

Gilman nodded. 'All right,' he said, 'so long as it don't interfere with the town you're welcome. We keep things quiet here. You enjoy yoreself an' don't make no fuss, you can have all the fun you want. Make trouble, an' you deal with me. Name's Gilman. George Gilman.'

'I'll remember that,' said Azul. 'Right now all I want is a stable an' a bed. You got any advice?'

'Try Mort Levy's place,' suggested Gilman. 'He charges kinda high, but it's the only stable around. Two blocks down to the alley, he's got a sign on the southside.'

'Thanks,' said Azul. 'How about someplace to sleep?'

Gilman shrugged. 'The Tucson Queen's got beds, but so's Levy. You want a quiet night I'd recommend the Virginia Palace. Levy owns that, too.'

Azul nodded his thanks and headed the tired black up

the street. The morning was time enough to ask about Nolan.

Gilman and Lyle watched him go, pacing out from the boardwalks to meet dead centre of mainstreet.

'How you figger him, George?' Lyle asked. 'You think he's with that killer?'

Gilman shrugged again.

'Can't rightly say, Lyle. He could be; then again, maybe not. Let's wait an' see. Give him the benefit o' the doubt.'

'Hardcase,' opined the deputy. 'He got the look o' a killer.'

'Don't make snap judgements,' cautioned Gilman. 'He got me kinda edgey, but I ain't pronouncin' no verdict on him. Not until he proves the case. He puts a foot wrong an' we come in like a steel edged trap. Until then it don't do no good to brood.'

CHAPTER FIVE

Azul checked the horse into the stablè, handing over five dollars for the stall and grain with a rub-down thrown in. It was a price over the going odds, but he felt too tired to argue. He handed over the coin and asked directions to the associated hotel.

It was situated opposite the stable, a two-storey place with a false front pegged on to the flat roof and a flourishing sign painted over the sun-bleached boarding.

Inside, it lost some of its pretensions. There was a double door with tinted glass panels opening on to a wide foyer that gave off a decrepit smell of musty carpet and stale spittoons. Most of the odour came from the faded red rug covering the floor. It might, once, have had a pattern, but that was long gone under a procession of bootheels and cigar butts, so that the covering now resembled nothing more than a patch of colourless wasteland. There was a central ring of buttoned velvet seats, their arms cut and curved to form a circle around the inner stand, decorated with a fancy pot of chipped blue china. A wilting plant spread tired leaves over the seats.

Three chairs of the same faded red colour as the carpet were set against the farther wall, and two high-back wooden loungers flanked the door. Off to the left was a bow-fronted desk with a pot plant fighting a losing battle against the stale air and a clerk who looked like he was doing the same with life. He had a thatch of black hair greased back from a wide, frown-creased forehead, and a pair of thin-rimmed spectacles perched midway down a flabby nose. His lips were thick and shiny with spittle, fashioning an automatic smile as his myopic gaze registered an incoming customer.

Azul walked over to the desk and dropped his carbine on the stained veneer.

The clerk looked at him, mouth pursing into an expression midway between smile and sneer.

'Sorry,' he said, 'but we don't have a room.'

Azul took a deep breath, controlling the anger he felt rising into action. He had been through this scene before: too many times to feel surprised. A whiteman could walk in looking like he'd just crawled through a cess pit, and get a room as soon as he showed some money. A Mexican – with a little more difficulty – could do the same. A half-breed, or an Indian, got the rush.

He peeled a ten dollar note from his vest. Spread it flat on the desk's top.

The clerk spread the sneer wider over his face and shook his head. Azul set a second bill over the first.

'We still don't have a room.' The man adjusted his glasses. 'We're booked real solid. No rooms free at all.'

Azul looked at the keyboard nailed to the wall behind

the desk. There were thirty hooks. Half were empty, the others all held keys.

'Don't you like money?' he asked quietly. 'I'll pay the goin' rate.'

'Sure I like it.' The clerk dropped his hands under the rim of the desk. 'But I got the privilege of deciding who I take it from.'

'An' you don't like takin' it from half-breeds or Indians,' grunted Azul.

'Or niggers.' The man jutted a thumb sideways, pointing at a notice pinned to the far wall. 'I'm real particular about them.'

Azul turned, reading the sign.

The Virginia Palace, it read, *is a respectable hotel. No whores allowed. No blacks. No Indians. No guns to be fired inside the rooms.*

'It doesn't mention half-breeds,' said Azul; quietly.

'Don't matter,' grunted the clerk. 'Half-breeds is the same as injuns or niggers.'

Azul nodded: 'Sure. I see your point.'

'Good.' The clerk's hands stayed under the desk. 'You could maybe get a stall down at the stable. Otherwise there's a hayloft out by the rail tracks.'

Azul grinned. It was a cold, ugly smile. He lifted the Winchester off the desk and turned away. He held the carbine by the forwards extension of the stock, fingers curled through the long hook of the lever, thumb passed over and round the hammer, holding it down. He turned and went on turning. The carbine swung out like a metal addition to his arm, arcing back over the desk with the full force of his spinning body behind it.

The barrel caught the clerk along the side of his jaw. The force of the blow snapped his head sideways, jerking his glasses loose on to the desk. The foresight snagged his cheek, leaving a thin line that began to drip blood over his faded shirt.

Azul halted his swing, bringing the carbine back to ram the muzzle into the man's chest. The clerk groaned and tottered backwards. Azul dropped the Winchester and reached out to hook both hands under the arms of the clerk's waistcoat. He yanked the man forwards across the desk, dragging him out so that he hung for a moment with his toes balanced on the veneer top and his hands scrabbling desperately at his throat. Then he opened his fists and let go.

The clerk thudded heavily on to the carpet and the faded plush got suddenly red where his teeth cut into his lower lip.

Azul let him fall, stepping over to the desk and reaching under the top to the shelf below. His hand closed on a length of cold metal and he pulled a shotgun into sight. The barrels were cut down to little more than nine inches and the stock was filed and cut to a pistol grip. He tripped the holding lever and ejected the cartridges, then tossed the scattergun to the far side of the room.

He grabbed the clerk by the front of his shirt and hauled him bodily over the carpet, yanking him on to his feet in front of the notice.

'No blacks?' he said.

The clerk's head rammed forwards and he spat blood over the paper.

'No Indians?'

The clerk's nose left a sticky smear across the wall.

'Respectable?'

The man slumped, a long trail of blood sliming down from the notice to where his face rested against the dirty wallpaper. His breath came in bubbling gasps that frothed crimson balloons from nostrils and mouth, and the mark of Azul's carbine stood black against the pallor of his skin.

The half-breed stepped back to the desk and picked up the Winchester. Then he went round behind and lifted a key from the nearest hook. He left the twenty dollars on the desk.

As he turned away the outer door swung open and Gilman came through.

The lawman had his shotgun pointed into the room

and a wary expression on his face. Lyle Watson backed him from the door.

'What in the goddam hell's happenin'?' demanded the sheriff. 'I thought I told you not to make no trouble?'

'Not me,' Azul grunted. 'All I wanted was a room. He made the trouble.'

'How come?' asked Gilman. 'Why the fight?'

'Seems he's prejudiced,' said Azul evenly. 'He objects to the blood in a man's veins.'

'Christ!' Gilman stared at the desk clerk's face and the crimson streamers decorating the wall. 'You surely don't.'

'It's all the same colour,' said Azul. 'Same as money.'

Gilman looked over to the two greenbacks on the desk. 'You offered to pay him that much?' he asked.

'It's there ain't it?' shrugged Azul. 'He argued about takin' it.'

'Man as argues over honest money is a damn' fool,' grunted the sheriff. 'You want the room still, you go ahead an' take it. I'll speak to Mort come mornin'. Maybe I'll talk some sense into him.'

'Thanks,' said Azul. 'That'd be a whole lot nicer than having him come after me with that shotgun.'

Gilman sniffed and picked up the sawed-off Meteor, tucking it under his belt. He called for Lyle to spread Mort Levy over the nearest sofa and left the hotel, pausing at the door to give Azul one final warning.

'No more trouble; all right?' His eyes looked disturbed. 'I ain't blamin' you fer this, but next time round watch out.'

'Sure.' Azul nodded. 'I don't want trouble any more than you.'

The way he said it got Gilman worried all over again.

Azul forgot the whole thing as he went upstairs to the room he had chosen. It faced on to mainstreet with a wide spread of double window affording clear view on both sides. The door had a bolt on the inside frame that he pushed shut and the bed looked wide and comfortable. There was a table with a jug of water and a bowl set against the wall. He stripped off his clothes and washed his face. Then he climbed under the sheets and went to sleep.

Tomorrow was soon enough to find Nolan. And he already had enough trouble in Tucson to worry about.

His last thought was of Carmady and why the Pinkerton hadn't ridden north to carry out his own investigation.

The next day he found out.

CHAPTER SIX

There was an Apache saying, taught him in his youth by the *rancheria*'s shaman. It said that the wise man was clever enough to get others to work for him. Azul realised the veracity of the proverb at the same time he realised that Carmady had bought a cheap five hundred dollars' worth of labour.

He left the hotel early after sun up and went to find a bath house. There was a place set back from the street a few buildings down from the Virginia Palace, run by the usual Chinese. A dollar bought him a hot tub and a guarantee of fresh-washed clothes while he soaked.

He enjoyed the bath after the nights on the trail up from Tubac and lay there for over an hour. It was a whiteman's fallacy about Indians being dirty: a misconception based on skin odours and eating habits. Most Indians bathed as much – often more – than the *pinda-lick-oyi,* using streams and springs whenever possible.

It made sense because an unbathed warrior might give his position away through the smell of his body; and a wound left unclean would fester and kill. Indians bathed. Enjoyed the luxuriance of water and soap. They might smell to a whiteman, though the odour would be that of food or rawhide rather than dirt, in the same way a whiteman would smell different to an Indian.

It was a cultural division accented, in Azul's mind and being, by his twin streams of blood. He had grown up alongside the Chiricahua full-bloods of his mother's people, learned their ways, become an Apache warrior descended from the great Mangas Colorado. At the same time his father had taught him to speak the tongue of the whiteman, had schooled him in the language and the ways of the *pinda-lick-oyi.*

So it was that he belonged to the two races, both red and white. He could understand both sides, sympathise with both as the white strain and the native red fought for supremacy. He could see why the whiteman sought to own the land and why the free warriors sought to fight them.

He was caught between, belonging to them both without finding trust in either camp.

White and red understood only their own needs, the daily exigencies of survival. On the one side stood the open plains and the buffalo, the need – desire – to roam free unencumbered by law or rails or telegraph wires, by towns or fences. Opposed to that was the whiteman's need for order. For law and structured divisions of the land. Which meant townships and fences; railroads and telegraph lines. Ranch buildings, windmills, stage depots.

The ordered lines of civilisation. The lines that came neat together on a map that was drawn up thousands of miles away and traced in by clerks who never saw the country they were dividing up and taking away from the free people who had fought for it, and won it.

It was easy to split a country by stroking a pen down a map. A map was no more than a sheet of paper; not the people on it. Like the mountains and the plains, they were nothing more than ciphers on the survey.

Figures to be assessed and dismissed into reservations.

The Indian lived with the land, the whiteman on it. Possessions meant little to the redmen – a decent pony, serviceable weapons, a blanket to keep out the night cold. An Indian village was a transient thing, constructed from the materials the country offered. It could disappear in hours and show up miles distant, wherever the seasons and the bounty of the land took the tribe. Not so the white towns of wood and stone that, once built, stayed. The inhabitants might go from the place, but the structures remained, markers of the white presence.

And now the open country was getting fenced in. Not with wire or wood, but with the more subtle, more devastating confinement of railroads and telegraph wires, townships and ranches. The buffalo grew fewer with each passing year, and the land itself began to change beneath the onslaught of cattle and traffic and ploughs. The free peoples of the south-west found themselves bound in by rules they neither understood nor recognised, but rules that were enforced with all the fearsome power of white organisation, backed by the industrial strength of the east. The whitemen appeared as a great river flooding out from the western banks of the Mississippi, drifting towards the place where the sun went down beyond the farther edge of the world. And they brought guns with them, cartridges, ploughshares, nails, saws, hammers: all the accoutrements of their civilisation that was so directly opposed to the free ways of the First People.

Azul knew that it must happen as surely as he knew that the sun must cross the sky and bring back the darkness. It was a blessing and a curse, laid upon him by the duality of his blood. He could understand the whiteman's driving need to establish himself in what he saw as a hostile land without condoning the manner of the coming. And at the same time he understood the need of the Indian to live free, following the old ways.

His grandfather, Mangas, had sought to find a path between, but that was too narrow a trail to walk in safety and Mangas had died at the hands of the *pinda-lick-oyi.* Kieron Gunn had sought to find the same path, and he had died because there was a bounty on Apache scalps.

The thought soured Azul's enjoyment of the bath and he stood up, shouting for cold water.

A Chinaman appeared with two big buckets. Azul sluiced his body down and dried himself. Then, dressed and feeling clean for the first time in three days, he went to look for Nolan.

Gilman was brewing coffee on a pot-bellied stove set against one wall of the jail. A sleepy-eyed deputy was cleaning out a rifle across the small outer office. Both men looked oddly nervous when he walked in.

'Mornin',' grunted Gilman. 'Want some coffee?'

Azul nodded: 'Thanks.'

He took the chair Gilman offered and sipped the coffee. It was black and bitter, the kind that wakes a man up and leaves a coating on his teeth.

'What can I do fer you?' Gilman asked. 'Mort try to throw you out again?'

'No.' Azul shook his head. 'I'm lookin' for information. About a man called Nolan. Tall man, with dark hair an' green eyes. Dresses mostly in black, an' he's fast with a gun. Got a temper to match.'

Gilman's face stayed calm, but his coffee mug got set down on the desk beside his left hand. His right went under, out of sight. Azul heard the dull *click* of a shell going into the loading gate of the fresh-cleaned Winchester. Then the triple *click* of lever and hammer. The back of his neck prickled with anticipation, but he resisted the urge to turn round and face the weapon pointed at his back.

'How come you're askin'?' Gilman's voice was flat, businesslike. 'He a friend o' yours?'

Azul shook his head. 'No. I was hired to find him.

Man in Tubac paid me five hundred dollars to locate him.'

Gilman whistled.

'Christ!' he said. 'That's two months pay fer me. What are you? A bounty hunter?'

'No,' murmured Azul. 'I'm not. I got a personal score with Nolan. The money's something else.'

'This feller in Tubac?' Gilman's hand came back into view filled with a Colt's Peacemaker that he set down on the desk next to his cup. 'He wouldn't be a big feller in a grey suit? Matching derby an' face that looks kinda tired? Around forty, but well preserved?'

Azul nodded, wondering what Carmady had talked him into.

Gilman chuckled.

'The Pinkerton,' he said. 'He was askin' questions a few days ago. When he got the answers he rode out. So he sent you back to try again.'

'So you know about Nolan,' said Azul, quietly. 'Where is he?'

Gilman smiled and ducked his head back at the door leading into the cell-block. 'In there. Held in custody until I get word outta Yuma. He killed a whore called Margie Robbins. Real hardcase. He figgered she'd robbed him, so he shoved her under a train. I reckon the theft'll mitigate his sentence, but he's down for ten or fifteen whichever way you look at it.'

Azul kept his face straight, showing no emotion despite the sudden flood of fear that prompted him to fight through and kill Nolan while he could. If the scalp-hunter got shipped up the line to the Yuma penitentiary he was lost behind the high stone walls and the guns.

White justice was one thing; Apache vengeance demanded a harder penalty, one paid out in blood and pain.

And Nolan owed him that.

'Can I see him?' asked Azul.

'Sure,' said Gilman, 'why not? You come a long way fer nuthin', so the least I can do is give you sight.' He set his big hand down over the Colt. 'O' course you'll hafta leave the gun out here. The knives, too.'

Azul nodded and reached down to unfasten the cord holding the holster tight against his thigh. He unbuckled the belt and swung it round the back of his chair. Then he lifted the throwing knife from his right moccasin and set it carefully on the desk.

Something hard and cold that he recognised as the muzzle of a Winchester dug into his back, just above the waist. Gilman stood up and came out from behind the desk. The big lawman sloped his hands over Azul's body, running them down ribs and waist, checking the legs – outside and inner thighs. He tested the moccasins, then back and arms.

'Guess you're clean,' he said. 'Go in an' talk. Nolan's at the back. Last cell along.'

Azul walked out from the desk and pushed the door to the cell-block open. Three steps led down to a stone floor flanked by cages that were mostly empty. Two were occupied by men with stubbled faces and the sour smell of too much cheap whisky. There was an acid smell of spilled urine and clouds of hungry flies. Beyond the corridor of cells there was a door. Azul went through and saw Nolan.

The dark man was stretched out on his bunk, arms cradling his head and his boots hooked through the bars of the outer wall.

Azul kicked the heels clear of the metal.

Nolan woke up looking angry. Then he laughed. It was a cold, ugly sound.

'Well,' he smiled, 'look what crawled in. A goddam half-breed. You took a long time catchin' up, boy.'

Azul stared at him, his eyes cloudy with rage. Nolan stood up, taking a position just far enough from the bars to be out of reach.

'Guess it makes you kinda mad to find me like this.'

He chuckled and spat. The gobbet hit the floor between Azul's feet. The half-breed didn't notice it: his eyes were fixed on Nolan's face. Unconsciously, he touched his left forearm, running his hand over the ridges of scar tissue cut there by his oath-taking. Cut there by his own knife as he looked down at the bodies of his mother and father and swore to kill their murderers.

'What happened to Jude?' asked Nolan. 'You catch up with him, too?'

'He's dead.' Azul's voice was throaty, the guttural Apache accent very strong. 'I killed him slow. Took his hair. The same way as I'll take yours.'

'Not in here, boy,' laughed Nolan. 'I got protection here.'

'You won't be in here all your life,' grated Azul.

'What you gonna do?' Nolan's voice was contemptuous, sneering. 'You gonna wait for me? All those years I'll be in the Yuma pen?'

Azul nodded. 'Yeah. It don't matter how long, nor where you are. I'll be there. Always.'

'Ain't it nice to know someone cares,' jeered Nolan. 'Maybe I should give you a reminder.'

He reached inside his jacket and tugged something out into the light. It was a hank of hair, long and silver-grey, attached to a dried out scrap of leathery skin.

Azul's eyes opened wide, blazing. His teeth clamped tight together and his lips got thin. His hands flexed, the fingers curving claw-like, like the talons of a predatory beast. His nostrils flared and a low moaning – a snarl – rumbled deep in his throat.

'Recognise it?' said Nolan. 'You should: it belonged to yore father. Ole Kieron had a fine head o' hair. Pity I couldn't sell it along with yore mother's.'

The snarl became a bellow. A tortured scream of rage and hate and frustration. Azul hurled himself against the bars, reaching through, fighting to shove his arms deep enough into the cell to grasp Nolan's throat.

The dark man laughed and jumped back, whisking the scalp over the clutching hands.

For a while Azul fought the bars, wolf-wild, oblivious

of anything but the need to sink his fingers into Nolan's windpipe. A door opened behind him. Then arms went around his chest and he was lifted up and back. He fought, ramming elbows and head against the man behind him. The grip loosened and he kicked out. Felt his heel slam against a leg and heard a grunt, the sound of a heavy body falling. He threw himself at the bars again. Nolan laughed. There was the thud of running feet. A shout. Something slammed hard against Azul's temple and he tasted blood in his mouth. There was a second blow. He felt his knees give way and clutched the bars. A third blow dropped him to the floor.

The last thing he saw was Nolan laughing as he dangled the scalp of Kieron Gunn derisively in front of the half-breed's bloodied face.

He woke to the sudden shock of cold water and tried to sit up.

He couldn't, and when he opened his eyes he realised that he was tied down to a chair in the outer office. Gilman stood over him and there was a deputy with a pistol levelled on his chest.

'You want him pretty bad,' said the lawman.

Azul spat blood from his mouth and nodded. The movement hurt his head.

'Yes,' he said. 'I do. That scalp he was waving was my father's.'

'Christ! So that's who you are.' Gilman sounded surprised. 'I shoulda recognised you straight off. I must be gettin' old.'

'Name's Gunn,' said Azul. 'Matthew Gunn.'

'Breed!' The deputy spoke in a shocked whisper. 'What do we do with him, George?'

'Nuthin',' grunted Gilman. 'He ain't wanted here an' I don't aim to take on more trouble than I need. We'll ride him outta town an' let him go.'

'I'll come back,' rasped Azul. 'I want Nolan.'

'Sure,' said the lawman, 'I can understand that. It's why I ain't holdin' you fer assault on a peace officer.

But you ain't gettin' Nolan. He's got a date with the judge in Yuma, an' I'm shippin' him out on the noon train tomorrow. Don't get no ideas, because he'll be under guard an' if you try anythin' you'll get yoreself killed.'

He stepped round behind the chair and untied the ropes. Azul climbed to his feet.

'We got yore horse outside,' said Gilman, 'so me an' Bob'll just escort you outta town. Don't try to come back.'

The two peace officers stepped aside and ushered Azul from the jail. Gilman carried his gunbelt and the throwing knife, the deputy held his Winchester. Azul climbed on to the black and rode out with the lawmen a safe distance behind him. They went out of Tucson on the north side and stopped about five miles into the scrub. Gilman threw the belt over and the deputy dropped the carbine on the sand.

'Remember what I said,' warned the big sheriff. 'You're posted in Tucson. Show yore face again an' it'll get blowed off.'

He turned his mount around and cantered away to the south.

Azul watched him go, then picked up the gunbelt. He buckled it on and thumbed fresh cartridges into the emptied Colt. He checked the Winchester and found that unloaded, too. Fast, his mind racing, he shoved new shells into the long gun. Then he sheathed the throwing knife and pulled the Bowie from the scabbard. There was dried-out mesquite all around and he used the knife to cut the feathery branches. After a while he had enough to make a decent fire. He damped the tinder with water from his canteen and set a match to the core.

After a while a thin column of dark smoke began to rise high through the clear morning air. Azul dragged his saddle blanket off the pony and spread it over the smouldering fire. He eased the blanket off of the wood, then spread it back, sending staggered streamers of the smoke lofting into the blue. He kept it up for thirty minutes or so, then hunkered down, waiting.

Waiting was all he could do for now.

Raul Granos approached Tucson from the south. He rode a solid-built bay gelding that resented the drag of the pack mule strung behind. When the horse skittered, the silver trappings of Raul's ornate saddle and harness set up a faint tinkling, like tiny bells.

The Mexican was a handsome man in his mid-forties, his face stubbled with the growth of a new beard. A thin knife scar showed white through the stubble on his right cheek. He wore an outfit to match his saddle gear. Tight black pants with big silver conchos down the sides covered tooled boots, dusty now from the long ride up out of Chihuahua. There were heavy spurs on the boots. The pants were held up by a narrow belt with a snake motif picked out in silver thread that showed beneath the waist of the high-cut jacket, itself picked out with the same fancy stitching at cuffs and chest. He wore a high, curly-brimmed sombrero. His only visible weapon was a late-model Winchester with silvered studs decorating the stock.

The mule was loaded with a heavy pack wrapped in oilskin and tied carefully to the wooden packsaddle.

Raul Granos looked tired and irritable.

When he got into Tucson he headed straight for the jail and hitched his horse outside. He removed his sombrero as he stepped into the office and fixed a friendly smile on his face.

Lyle Watson looked up from the dodgers he was studying and wondered what the Mexican wanted.

'Buenas dias,' murmured Raul. 'It may be that you can help me. I am looking for a man called Nolan.'

'Why?' asked Lyle, easing back to rest one hand on the Colt at his hip. 'What you want with him?'

Raul smiled some more and shrugged. 'Business, *señor*. A private matter. Do you know where I can find him?'

'Sure do,' grinned the deputy, 'only he ain't receivin' no more visitors. Don't figger he'll be talkin' to no one fer a while. We got him in the cells. You want to speak to him, you'll hafta go up to Yuma an' wait fer visitin' day. Sheriff's orders.'

'Madre de Dios!' The smile left Raul's face for a moment. 'It appears I have come a long way for nothing.'

'I guess so,' said Lyle. 'Sorry.'

'De nada.' Raul turned away, thinking hard. *'Adios, señor.'*

He left the office and climbed back on the bay. Conscious of the deputy watching him from the doorway, he rode off down the street. He went to the far end of mainstreet and swung the gelding into a side alley. A secondary track bisected the alley at right angles, flanked by little frame houses and a scattering of storage sheds. He followed the track back, riding parallel to mainstreet. Twice he was forced to detour, but after a while he knew that he was close to the rear of the jail. He dismounted and hitched the gelding to a stunted plane tree, then walked softly down to the nearest window. Reaching up, he tapped a beringed fist against the bars.

Nolan's face appeared.

'Granos?'

'*Si.* You are Nolan?'

'Yeah.' The dark man ducked back, listening for a moment. 'We're safe to talk fer now, but I ain't got long.'

'You would seem to have plenty of time,' murmured Raul cynically. 'And I have wasted some of mine.'

'You ain't wasted nuthin',' whispered Nolan. 'Not if you do like I tell you.'

'Señor.' The Mexican's formality was tinged with sarcasm. 'I got word that you sought a printer. That you would pay twenty thousand dollars to the right man. That offer was tempting enough to bring me from Chihuahua – to find you in jail. What deal can you offer when you are behind bars?'

'A goddam good deal,' snarled Nolan, 'but it depends on you gettin' me out.'

Raul laughed quietly. 'I am a printer, not a jail breaker, Nolan.'

'Hell, Mex! ' Nolan fought to control his anger. 'Will you listen to me? You already got five hundred: that should buy a little time.'

The Mexican smiled and began to polish his rings against his shirt. 'All right,' he sighed. 'But be swift. I have no desire to join you inside.'

'See if this convinces you,' grunted Nolan. 'I got sixty thousand dollars in my saddlebags an' two Government printin' plates with my other gear. The sheriff ain't checked it out yet, but they're gonna do that fer sure when I get to Yuma. If they do, they'll know where it come from. You help me bust out an' we split down the middle. That change yore mind any.'

Raul whistled softly, and his eyes got wide and bright; interested.

'What must I do?'

'They're shippin' me to Yuma at noon tomorrow,' whispered Nolan. 'There'll be guards ridin' shotgun all the way an' I reckon they'll most likely put me in the brake car. You get on the train an' bring me a gun. There won't be more'n three deputies; maybe a brake-man. We kill them an' jump.'

'With your belongings,' murmured Raul.

'O' course.' Nolan saw that he had the Mexican hooked. 'Then we head back across the border an' set to work.'

'Very well.' Raul smiled. 'I am with you . . . partner.'

He turned away, then paused. '*Hasta luego, amigo.* I will see you tomorrow. On the train.'

'Christ! I hope so,' muttered Nolan, climbing down off the bunk. 'I sure hope so.'

Raul Granos went back to his horse and rode round to mainstreet again. He got himself a room in the Tucson Queen and a bottle of whisky. He left the bay and the mule in Levy's stable and took a hacksaw and sanding blocks from the pack. He cast a regretful look at the fancy saddle, knowing that it was the last time he would see it. Then he cheered up at the thought of buying an even better rig with his share of the money. After that he bought a single-barrel Remington shotgun, two Colt's Frontier models, and shells for all three weapons. Then he went back to his room and opened the bottle.

He drank one glass staring at the Remington, then set the shotgun down on the table and began to saw through the barrel. It was difficult without the aid of a vice, but Granos was accustomed to trimming metal and cut through after thirty odd minutes. He held the gun between his knees and buffed the muzzle smooth. Then he set it back on the table and cut the shoulder piece away. It took him a couple of hours to cut and sand the pistol grip smooth until the weapon sat comfortably in his hands, but when he was finished he had a lethal weapon that could be easily hidden beneath his clothing. The barrel was cut down almost to the fore-grip and the shotgun resembled a single-shot pistol. It would have an effective accuracy of little more than six or seven feet, but within that range it would devastate anything in the path of the ought-gauge shot. He checked the mechanism and slid the gun into his pants. His jacket hid the grip and the material of his trousers, although bulked out, concealed the barrel effectively enough.

He drank a second glass of whisky and tucked the two Colts under his belt, at the small of his back. There was a full-length mirror inside the wardrobe and when he craned his head round he thought the revolvers were well enough hidden. Sitting was awkward with the two pistols and impossible with the Remington.

Raul swore fluently, wondering how to overcome the problem.

Then he got an idea and went back to the stable. He removed a saddle strap from the mule's load and took it up to the room. The strap was about one inch wide and five feet long. He cut it down to a manageable size and tied it to the grip and forepiece. Then he removed his jacket and slung the loop over his right shoulder. With the strap hiked up to settle the Remington against his back and his jacket on, the scattergun was concealed.

He spent an hour practising drawing the gun. When he was satisfied, he took another drink and loaded all three weapons before hiding them under his mattress. He brushed the filings of wood and metal into the cracks between the floorboards and shoved the stock behind the wardrobe.

He washed his hands and face and went looking for food. He felt nervous as all hell and drank a lot with his meal. Raul Granos was no gunfighter and had scant relish for the next day's work. But money was money, and greed was a great cure for fear.

Raul Granos went to sleep with the thought of thirty thousand dollars and two printing plates in his mind.

While Raul worked, Azul waited.

He waited with the tireless patience of an Apache warrior, squatting in the shade of a big saguarro with his eyes wandering over the horizons.

After a while movement showed and Azul climbed to his feet. He took off his stetson and reached down to his belt, unwinding a narrow cord of rawhide. He fastened the cord around his head, tying back his hair.

The cord was the war band of the Chiricahua; a symbol that would – he hoped – be recognised by the approaching riders.

He hunkered down again, chewing slowly on a strip of dried meat. His Winchester was rested across his knees, the Colt loose in the holster.

He watched the horsemen come closer. Waiting.

CHAPTER SEVEN

The riders halted a half-mile out from his fire, watching.

Then they split up and spread out. In seconds two of them were gone from sight, using the hollows and the sparse vegetation to cover their progress. A progress he knew would bring them to him on either side. The third rode straight in.

He was a short, ugly man with a broken nose and shoulder-length black hair hanging in greasy folds from his headband. He rode a pinto mustang with a pad saddle and carried a .50 calibre Sharps canted over the pony's shoulders. Azul saw that the hammer of the buffalo gun was cocked.

'Greetings,' he said. 'Will you talk with me?'

The Apache stared at him, not moving. The big carbine was angled round to point at Azul's chest.

'There are two guns ready to take your life,' he said. 'They are the fast-firing kind the whiteman use. But they are not really necessary: I could kill you now.'

'I know,' said Azul. 'But why should you? I sent smoke to call you. I speak your tongue because my mother was Rainbow Hair af the Chiricahua, daughter to Mangas Colorado.'

'Hai! So you are the one called Azul.' The hammer of the Sharps set down with an audible *click*. 'I have heard much about you. I am Lame Pony of the Ojo Caliente.'

'I greet you, brother,' said Azul. 'Will you join me and take coffee?'

'Whisky would taste better,' grunted Lame Pony, 'but I will join you anyway. Hey!' he gestured to the hidden braves. 'Naza! Fox Runner! Come here and drink coffee.'

Azul listened to the sound of the approaching mustangs. He took care not to turn round, simply waiting until both warriors dismounted and chose to show themselves. Naza was a tall buck in a faded red shirt and a Cavalry kepi. He looked nervous and kept his Winchester close beside him even though he smiled a greeting and thanked Azul for the offer of coffee. Fox Runner was older, dressed in a mixture of white and Indian clothes. His torso was covered by a blue Army jacket with three holes across the chest, each one rimmed with a dull stain. He wore buckskin leggings with a breech-clout covering the crotch, where the seat was cut away. There was a Cavalry belt around his waist, holding an old Colt's Dragoon and a long-bladed knife.

Like Lame Pony, both Naza and Fox Runner wore gaudy cloth wound about their heads.

'You have the war band,' said Lame Pony. 'Why?'

Azul reached out to lift the coffee pot from the fire. He filled his mug and passed it over.

'You know my name,' he said as Lame Pony sipped and passed the tin cup on to Fox Runner. Azul noticed the hierarchy. 'So you know that my rancheria was destroyed by white scalphunters.'

'It has been told,' said Lame Pony. 'Also that you follow the white ways to avenge the killing.'

Azul nodded. 'Yes. I have hunted the killers a long time now. And I have found them. And killed them.'

'That is good.' Fox Runner and Naza grunted their agreement. 'So why did you summon us?'

'There is one who still lives,' said Azul. 'He is called Nolan and he is held prisoner in the jail in Tucson. This morning he waved my father's scalp in my face and laughed at me.'

Lame Pony turned his head aside and spat. Naza grunted and thumped a clenched fist against his naked thigh. Fox Runner made the devil sign.

'That is bad,' said Lame Pony. 'It is bad that the whitemen come and take our country away and kill us when we fight them. To offend a man with the hair of his father is an insult that must be answered. We shall help you. I can summon thirty men willing to settle this matter. What shall we do? There are many guns in Tucson, but I think we could raid the whiteman jail and kill this hunter of hair.'

'No.' Azul shook his head. 'If you did that the whites would bring the soldiers against you and kill your rancherias as they did mine. This thing rests between me and the one called Nolan. I must kill him myself. I made that promise to my father and my mother.'

He unbuttoned his sleeve and rolled the cloth up to expose the scars.

'I took blood oath on this. He must die by my hand alone.'

The Apaches nodded their assent, grunting appreciation of his undertaking.

'We shall help you,' said Lame Pony. 'What would you have us do?'

Azul passed the coffee cup round again. 'The man leaves Tucson on the train that departs when the sun is highest. He is being sent to the town called Yuma, where they will put him into the prison. I must get aboard that train and find him. Then I must take him off and kill him.'

'That will be difficult,' said Lame Pony. 'The trains go faster than a mustang and they are very hard to stop. Why not become a whiteman again and ride the thing from the stopping place? That would be easier.'

'No,' said Azul. 'The white law-giver has said that he will kill me if I go back to the town. He will be with the man called Nolan, and I should be foolish to risk dying before I can kill Nolan.'

'True,' grunted Lame Pony. 'What can we do then?'

'If something were to block the rails so that the train must halt, or slow down,' said Azul, 'it would give me a chance to climb on board. If I knew that two horses waited, I could take the man off and ride away.'

Lame Pony laughed, his ugly face splitting up into creased lines of appreciation.

Fox Runner slapped his leg and said: 'There are plenty of cows around here. They are fat for the winter on whiteman's grain and our grass. They would make a fine barrier.'

'And I could bring the ponies up,' said Naza. 'It would feel good to teach the whiteman a lesson.'

'So.' Lame Pony got serious. 'We shall do this, though I understand what you say about the Army. I think it might be better if no one else knows.'

'No one else needs to know,' said Azul. 'Three good brothers are enough.'

Lame Pony stood up. 'Then let us go,' he said. 'Better that we have our cows caught ready than hunt them tomorrow.'

Azul shucked the dregs from the coffee pot and swilled it with sand. He packed pot and mug back into his saddlebags and mounted the black pony after kicking dirt over the fire.

He rode away with a tight, menacing smile on his face.

Nolan felt uneasy after Raul Granos left him.

He didn't know the Mexican, or trust him. And the fancy-panted printer hadn't given any impression of knowing how to handle a gun. Nolan wondered if he would come through as promised. Greed was the obvious spur, but it might not be enough.

Nolan went to sleep wondering.

Raul went to sleep thinking about the money. He woke up five times and quelled his doubts with whisky. Killing wasn't his line, but he thought he could manage for that kind of reward.

Big George Gilman made his rounds wondering about

the scribbled message Lyle Watson had left him. He couldn't understand Lyle's writing at the best of times and with the deputy gone home to sleep out his off-duty spell, there was no way of telling what the note said.

Gilman hoped it didn't spell trouble. All he wanted right then was to get Nolan on the train with his two deputies to look after him on the way to Yuma.

Three, he figured, should be enough. Lyle and Bob and Will were reliable; and he had been on his feet for more than twenty hours. Goddam Breed! he thought. If he hadn't shown up so early, he could be in bed now instead of swapping duty with Lyle. Still, he could catch up in the morning.

Carmady rolled over in the big bed and stared at the ceiling.

Linda Velazquez was a warm huddle beside him, giving off a sweet-scented odour of perfume and wine and sex. On that score he had to allow the half-breed a debt of gratitude. If the 'breed got Nolan out of Tucson and brought him back he'd have more than earned his five hundred dollars. And five hundred out of two grand was a low investment. If the 'breed got the plates and the money, too, Carmady would be laughing.

All the way to Mexico City. Or maybe Europe.

Anyways, some place where Allan Pinkerton or anyone else couldn't find him.

Whatever the outcome, he stood to win. He slapped Linda on the rump and dragged her round to face him. Her arms opened in automatic welcome.

Carmady moved on to her, glad that her legs did the same.

Azul and the three Apaches rode west until they came to a low bluff facing on to the rail tracks. The scarp face went down into a tiny canyon with a stream spilling water over the rocks. There was grass at the bottom and a stand of piñon around the entrance.

It was a good place for cows to herd up, and there

was about seven head spread around the far end.

The Indians lifted *riatas* from their saddles. Azul's rope was made of hemp, but he knew how to use it.

They drifted slowly up the canyon. The cows lowed nervously, but by the time they realised what was happening four ropes had dropped over horns and necks and four fat steers were being dragged, protesting, out of the watering place.

The four men urged the cattle clear of the canyon, then across the night-swept desert to a buffalo wallow a quarter mile from the tracks.

They waited there until it was close to noonday, then led the cows out and haltered them to short tethers over the rails. Before the steers could panic and tear loose each man stepped up close and shot them between the eyes. The heavy bodies crumpled across the tracks, too many for the engine's cowcatcher to shove loose without stopping and backing up for several runs.

After that, Azul and the three Ojo Caliente warriors settled down to fix the next part of his plan. It was agreed that Naza and Fox Runner should go on ahead with the horses to where the train slowed for the gradient lifting over a ridge. Lame Pony would stay with Azul, then ride on to join the others. Should the half-breed need help, they would be close by.

Azul stared off down the tracks, waiting anxiously for the train to show.

'Thank you, my brothers,' he said as Naza and Fox Runner prepared to leave. 'Thank you for your help.'

'It is a good plan,' grinned Lame Pony. 'A plan that will teach the whitemen a lesson. They will not like it.'

'No,' murmured Azul. 'It is what they would call a bum steer.'

CHAPTER EIGHT

Nolan was escorted to the rail depot by Gilman, Bob Tucker and Will Hatch. All three lawmen carried shotguns; the deputies carried Nolan's gear. The dark man was unable to carry anything because his wrists were tied together behind his back.

The train was held up to let them board after the other passengers, so they never saw the Mexican with the curiously stiff back climb on board and take a seat at the rear of the last passenger car. They got into the brake van and locked the side door. The guard looked nervous as they settled down. He was fifty-two years' old and looking forward to a lazy retirement: he hoped there wouldn't be any trouble.

Gilman got his men settled down inside the small van and shoved Nolan into a corner. The brake car was wooden sided, with nothing in it except the machinery and a built-in desk with a fixed chair bolted to the floor in front of it. The lawmen lounged against the walls, facing their prisoner. Gilman untied Nolan's wrists and brought them round to the front. Then he looped the rope again, leaving about three feet spare to knot around a stanchion: he didn't like to see a prisoner suffer unnecessarily, not even one like Nolan.

Nolan smiled in what Gilman thought was gratitude. It wasn't: the killer was thinking about his chances of escape. He was thinking that Raul Granos would let the train gather speed for the upgrade that lifted the rails towards the Gila river and hit the brake car just before it hit the downslope. His hands were loose enough to clutch a gun, and with the element of surprise on their side it should be easy to kill the peace officers. They already had their shotguns down on the floor and a pack of cards out into play. If the Mexican timed his appearance right, they should be able to take out the lawmen and jump the train just before it picked up speed. The unloading would be tricky, but by the time the train got stopped it should be a long way down the slope. And Nolan would be a long way off into the open spaces.

He eased back against the wall and closed his eyes. He was still smiling.

Azul was thinking along the same lines.

The dead steers would block the train long enough for him to get on board. After that he needed to locate Nolan and get the scalphunter away from his escort. The best place for that manoeuvre was the point where the train slowed right down, then picked up speed again. He sent Naza and Fox Runner up with the two horses; Lame Pony stayed to see he got on board safely.

It was a simple plan, but the most effective he could think of. Once he had Nolan tied on a pony he could ride the dark man off into the Dragoons and kill him at leisure amongst the lonely crags.

He bellied up close to the rails, waiting.

Raul Granos sat quietly with a thin cheroot in his mouth and a nervous blankness pulling his eyes out of focus. He could feel the two Colts digging into his back and wondered why no one had questioned the strange bulking of his jacket. He sat up very straight, trying hard to look normal and unconcerned. It was difficult with Mrs Bixby's piercing grey eyes fixed on his face.

There were only three passengers in the car. One was Raul, the second a drummer in a grubby brown suit with a hip flask tucked into the inside pocket. The hip flask was empty now and the drummer was snoring softly with his legs spread over a full-length of seat. The third was Mrs Bixby.

Mrs Bixby was thirty-five years' old and a widow. She had mouse-brown hair dragged back in a loose bun under the rim of her tilted straw bonnet. She wore a high-necked white blouse with a jade brooch fastening the throat, and a drab suit that matched her drab hair. Her face was lined with the kind of wrinkles that come from disapproving of almost everything except Sunday School and abstinence. The frowns got deeper when she looked at the drummer, and her snubby nose turned up and got thin in contempt of the whisky fumes coming out with his snores. She didn't approve of Mexicans, either, but felt it her duty to patronise the lower species. She had tried to start a conversation with Raul.

When he replied to her bad Spanish with fluent English, she had puckered her lips and crinkled her nose and talked as though addressing a child. Raul had lit a cheroot.

Mrs Bixby had pointed out that she couldn't condone the inhalation of tobacco smoke.

Raul blew a nervous gust straight into her face.

Mrs Bixby stood up and coughed, waving a brown-gloved hand around her irritable face. Raul had smiled and murmured an apology. He let more smoke spill from his mouth while he said it.

Mrs Bixby found herself another seat and opened her bible. She didn't read much of it because her gaze was mostly centred on Raul. It was like being stared at by a vulture.

After a while he stood up and opened the door on to the rear platform.

Behind him he heard Mrs Bixby mutter something about it being a God-sent blessing to get free of filthy smoke in a voice loud enough to carry all the way down the car. He shut the door and leaned against the rail.

The brake van was facing him across three feet of rusting iron. There was a door with a handle on the outside and no sign of movement from within. Raul took a last gasp of his cheroot and flicked the stub out on to the sand. Then he licked his lips and waited for the train to slow.

He had come to the same conclusion as Nolan: that the best place to make the attack would be at the apex of the gradient. He waited; nervously.

Then he heard the whistle shrill off a warning and felt the car lurch; slowing. The connecting rods between the passenger wagon and the brake van trembled and he grabbed the observation rail with both hands to prevent himself from falling off.

The train stopped. Backed up. Went forwards again. The platform shook. The train backed. Slammed into something hard and heavy. Backed again. Shunted on, then picked up steam and moved upwards.

Raul lit a second cheroot and wished he had a drink.

Azul watched the engine approach the dead steers. Saw it slow with the big screamer mounted alongside the funnel howling a warning at the cows spread over the rails.

The Baldwin hit, pulping two carcases into bloody ruin. It backed up and took a second run. The first two steers were shoved clear; the third got caught on the cowcatcher and the engine reversed again. Then it went forwards and ploughed the last carcase off of the rails.

Azul lifted from the sand, racing towards the nearest ladder.

The engine shunted back, halted, and went on to clear the track. Azul grabbed a mounting rail and swung on to the frontside platform of the second passenger car. The train had only two cars between the engine and the brake van, and he guessed that Nolan would be held in the rear caboose.

He went up the ladder on to the roof.

The train picked up speed, threatening to shake him loose as he clambered on to the top of the passenger car. He grabbed hold of the ventilation funnels, peering back at Lame Pony as the Apache whooped and heeled his mount to a gallop northwards.

He clung tight until the train settled down a bit, then rose to his feet and worked his way slowly along the roof.

Waiting for the opportune moment, he bellied down flat a few feet from the rearward extension of the car, where he couldn't be seen by the passengers or the lawmen inside the brake van.

The engine gathered speed, gaining momentum for the run up the long gradient. Azul held tight and waited for the slowing down that would signal the time for action. When the train slowed it would be time. His Apache brothers would have the horses waiting. Then he would go down into the brake car and take Nolan.

Take him free: to die.

Raul Granos got too nervous to calculate the approach right.

He felt the rumble of the engine settle down to a steady pounding and sensed that it was gathering power. He wasn't used to trains, and so thought that the engine was mounting the gradient. He eased the cut-down shotgun out from his jacket.

Then Mrs Bixby appeared.

She swung the door open and stalked out on to the platform, glaring at the blank door of the brake car. Her bible was tucked away inside the poke bag slung over her left wrist and her thin lips were puckered down between her angry mutterings.

'Disgusting service,' she barked. 'I shall complain. No conductor. No service. No decency. A train full of dirty Mexicans and drunkards. Foul. Disgusting.'

She caught sight of Raul and swung round, the poke bag lifting up as the wind took it.

'You!' she snapped. 'You Mexican! What are you doing out here?'

Raul panicked.

He swung the Remington out on the leather strap and drove the cut-down barrel hard against Mrs Bixby's jaw. Blood splattered from her face and her eyes opened in outrage.

She swung her bag viciously at Raul's head.

The Mexican ducked, but the bag still caught him on the shoulder, knocking him off balance as the train swung into a curve. The bag was heavy, weighted down by the bible and Mrs Bixby's bottle of smelling salts.

Raul fell down on to the platform. Mrs Bixby swung the bag again. Raul lifted the shotgun and squeezed the trigger. The sound was carried away by the wind and the howling of the engine's whistle as it swung through the curve. The heavy-gauge shot hit Mrs Bixby at a range of three feet. It picked her up and bounced her off the door of the passenger car. Her mouth opened in surprise as her torso separated from her waist. Splintered shards of whalebone corset sprang loose from her bloodied dress and her legs crumpled, her body folding at an unnatural angle that draped the upper part of her corpse over the gap between the two cars.

Raul broke the shotgun open and fumbled a new shell into the breech.

He stood up and kicked the bloodstained bag from the platform. Then he looked at Mrs Bixby and vomited. He doubled over the rail, streaming trailers of bile down past the brake van.

After a while he pushed himself upright and looked at the door of the brake van. The sound of his shot had gone unnoticed. He made himself look at the body. After a moment's thought, he kicked it down between the two cars.

Mrs Bixby snagged on the link chain. Her legs dangled down, bumping and shredding against the rails and sleepers; her right arm hung over the edge of the platform, her left caught in the guard-rail of the brake van. Her head and torso jounced against the metal step of the caboose.

Raul stepped over on to the platform of the brake van and pounded on the door.

'Help!' He shouted. 'For God's sake, help! There's someone hurt. Come help her.'

He cocked the shotgun and tugged one Colt out, tucking it into his waistband. The other he clutched in his left hand. Then he kicked the door and shouted some more.

Inside the van George Gilman stood up, looking at the guard.

'Sounds like trouble,' he said. 'Best see what's happenin'.' He turned to his deputies. 'Will, you flank the door. Bob, keep yore gun on the prisoner.'

The brakeman swung the door open.

Raul Granos squeezed the trigger of the Colt as the blue uniform showed. The .45 bullet dug deep into Thomas Lipton's body and punctured his heart. It went on through and broke a rib coming out of his back, spending itself in the woodwork of his desk. He opened his mouth to scream, but the cry got all clogged up on the blood and he swung round into Will Hatch.

Raul tossed the Colt over to Nolan, swinging round to point the Remington inside the van and fire.

Nolan caught the thrown pistol as the shotgun went off. He saw the deputy called Will lift up and cannon back against Gilman with his head blown away along with most of his chest and shoulders.

Gilman shouted, lifting one hand to slap at his face where stray pellets were peppering blood from his cheeks. He twisted, dropping to the floor. Nolan saw that one eye was bloodied, blind where a lead ball had torn through the lower lid.

The scalphunter thumbed the hammer of the Colt, firing wild at Bob Tucker.

The deputy was caught between the falling body of his boss and the man at the door. Nolan's shot slammed into his neck before he could swing his Meteor back to level on the prisoner. The shotgun went off with a booming roar that spread a diamond pattern over the wall to Nolan's left. The Colt's bullet hit him in the throat, severing the carotid artery so that a thick fountain of crimson blood arced out sideways from his neck. Nolan's second shot hit his face. It entered to the left side of his nose, ricochetted off his teeth and spiralled up into his brain, gouting bone and bloodstained grey matter high into the air.

Raul Granos stepped inside the car with the Remington swinging wild from side to side.

Nolan saw the panic on the Mexican's face and huddled back into the corner.

Gilman rolled on to his knees. There was blood all down his shirt, smearing the brass star pinned to his chest. Blood ran from his eye and cheek, but he still had his pistol in his hand. He shook his head like a wounded bull and looked up. He had to turn his head sideways to see clearly and as he did so Raul fired the shotgun again.

The blast caught the peace officer full on the right side of his face. It stripped away his scalp and most of the skin on the cheek and temple and jaw. Bone showed white, then abruptly red, and Gilman's mouth dangled open where the tendons were severed. He dropped the Colt. His right eye stared at Nolan from out of a red mask and strangled sounds burst from his ragged lips.

Nolan grinned and took aim.

He fired at Gilman's right wrist, shattering the bone so that the lawman fell down on his side. The next bullet broke the left shoulder, leaving Gilman helpless on the floor.

Blood spilled from his face and body, but his glaring eye remained fixed on Nolan.

The dark man thumbed back the hammer. He chuckled as he sighted. Gilman's eye exploded as the .45 slug tore into the brain beyond and shattered the base of his skull. The sheriff collapsed like a punctured balloon filled with crimson liquor.

Nolan laughed.

'Hey, Mex,' he shouted, 'you did real good! Now come an' get me loose.'

Raul Granos doubled over and spewed bile he didn't know he still had inside him. When he was finished retching he cut Nolan loose and sat down on the chair. He jumped up when he felt something warm and sticky seeping through his pants and looked down: the seat was covered with blood.

'All right,' grunted Nolan, 'let's get the brake on an' slow this thing down. Best shut that door while you're at it.'

Raul staggered over to lock the connecting door, then went back to help Nolan with the brake. They locked it on and waited for the train to slow.

Nolan grinned, picking up his gear.

'Neat,' he said. 'Real neat. This way there ain't no one comin' after us. Time they sort out what happened here an' get the brake off, we'll be long gone.'

Raul nodded without speaking.

Up on the roof Azul felt the train begin to slow. He rose to his knees. Ahead he saw Naza lift the Winchester twice, indicating the presence of the horses. He lifted an arm in reply and crawled to the end of the car.

He swung down on to the observation platform and jumped across to the brake van. Gently, he tested the lock: the door was shut tight. He reached up to grasp the side-mounted ladder and climbed on to the roof. The train went on slowing as he ran along the swaying caboose to the rear end.

He climbed down and tested the door. It was unlocked.

He eased back the hammer of his Colt and kicked the door inwards.

Someone shouted and he felt the sting of shotgun pellets against his left arm and cheek. He fired blind and heard a man scream in anger.

Then there was the dull explosion of a handgun and he felt a terrific blow slam into his stomach. He doubled over, fighting the pain, but his feet skidded off the platform and he felt the wooden floor ram against his face.

He tasted blood in his mouth, then felt his feet hit the sleepers and begin to bounce. He fought to hold his grip on the rail, but the movement of the train was too much and his fingers slipped loose. He felt himself fall with that slowing of time that comes when the body senses danger and pumps adrenalin into the bloodstream so that objective time becomes a tortoise-movement compared to the acceleration of subjective activity.

He saw the train go away in front of him, then cartwheeled, watching his legs arc high across the sky. He felt the sleepers slam against his shoulders, his arms come down on to the rails. The world spun round as he rolled behind the departing train and he thought about how close he had come to getting Nolan.

Then his rolling movement stopped and his head slammed hard against a sleeper.

Light exploded with incandescent fury across his eyes and the world went dark and dead.

Nolan stood on the platform of the brake van, staring back at the tumbling body. He saw the spread of blood over the stomach and the way the loose limbs hit the rails.

I guess I killed him, he thought. *At last.*

He turned back inside and shouted for Raul to get ready to jump. The Mexican looked nervous about it, so Nolan tossed the saddlebags clear and then booted him off the platform.

Raul hit the sand with a heavy thump, rolled over, and sat up with a look of blank surprise on his face. Nolan sprang clear to land on both feet. He kept his body limp, letting himself fall into the shock, tumbling over on to his left shoulder and sprawling, unhurt, on the desert.

When he sat up he saw an Indian with a dirty Cavalry

cap on his black hair racing towards him with two horses in tow.

He cocked his pistol and waited for the Indian to get closer.

The Apache was in a hurry. By the time he halted his wild gallop the train was almost stopped and Nolan was pointing the Colt at his chest.

Naza saw the gun and realised his mistake too late.

Nolan's bullet hit him just below the clavicle. It blasted through the muscle covering Naza's stomach and broke his spine. The Ojo Caliente warrior tumbled backwards over his pony's tail as the mustang reared in surprise and Nolan ran forwards to seize the lead reins of the following horses.

Raul Granos opened his eyes and saw a screaming Apache in a faded Army coat racing towards him with a pistol blowing smoke over his pony's mane. Raul acted instinctively. He lifted the Remington and pulled the trigger. The pony's skull exploded in a back-flying welter of messy blood mingled with shards of bone and sticky, grey brain matter. It somersaulted, pitching its rider yards out over its missing head.

Raul stood up and ran back. When he reached the groaning Apache, he swung the Remington like a club. Like his pony's skull, Fox Runner's head was mashed.

Nolan shouted and Raul turned.

A third rider was coming in. The Mexican began to fumble a shell into the scattergun, then remembered the second Colt tucked into his waistband. He dropped the Remington and held the pistol out between both hands.

Nolan was holding on to the bucking horses and firing his own gun at the man. Raul cocked and aimed. Fired carefully. He felt numb, distanced from the action by the shock of the horrific killings on the train. He sighted on the Apache's stomach and squeezed the trigger. The bullet hit the man as the big carbine he was holding went off and plumed dust six inches from Raul's feet.

The Apache yelled and dropped the carbine. Raul fired again.

His second shot took the warrior off his horse when it was no more than three yards from the Mexican. The mustang went on running; Raul hurled himself out of its path. When he stood up the Apache was climbing to his feet with a knife in his right hand and his left clamped tight over the hole in his belly.

'Shoot him! Fer Crissakes shoot him! I got no more slugs!'

Nolan was still holding on to the horses, waving his empty gun as he shouted.

Raul fired. The Apache went down with blood on his face. The Mexican fired again. The Apache dropped his knife and tried to wipe the blood away from his eyes. Raul fired. He took no count of how many times until Nolan shouted at him and he realised the hammer was falling on empty cylinders.

The Apache was sprawled on the sand with blood all over his body and a spreading pool oozing out from under him.

Raul dropped the Colt and stumbled over to the horses.

'Christ! If I didn't need you to print fer me, I'd leave you here,' snarled Nolan. 'But I do need you, so let's get ourselves the hell outta here.'

They spurred away over the sand, heading south. Down towards the Santa Cruz river and the Mexican border. Down towards a safe hiding place where they could print all the money they'd ever need.

After a while Raul began to smile at the thought of it.

Behind them the train gathered speed.

Engineer and driver both agreed that they had wasted enough time stuck out in the wastelands of Arizona with crazy Apaches raiding the train and killers breaking loose. It could all be reported to the authorities in

Yuma. But right then, for the sake of the passengers, it was best to get clear. Fast.

The train left most of Mrs Bixby behind it. No one was very eager to scrape her clear, so she got left; except for her torso and head, which was put in the brake van along with the bodies of Gilman and his two deputies.

The dead Apaches were left on the sand. Buzzards and ants and coyotes could give them burial. It was no more than they deserved.

And not one of the crew or passengers noticed the body sprawled on the side of the tracks a quarter mile back.

Azul's stetson was two yards away, the crown damp and browned with blood. His yellow hair blended into the sand, except where a black column of flies supped busily on the matted crimson that welled thick from his sun-bleached mane. Ants scurried to the blood oozing from his stomach, and buzzards hovered high above, waiting for the noisy engine to go away.

His hand was still clenched tight on the butt of his Colt, but his face was down on the ground. Still and silent and death-like.

The train pulled out and the buzzards began to spiral downwards. One dead horse was feast enough; four dead men was luxury.

CHAPTER NINE

A wolf howled, baying a greeting to the rising moon.

It was a lonesome, hungry sound, full of emptiness and longing. It echoed over the prairie, sending the coyotes and the prairie dogs running for cover. The buzzards and vultures sitting heavy on the rails flapped their wings and squawked a protest at the interference. The wolf howled again. The birds crowed a raucous objection and lifted into the growing dark, hurrying to find safe perching places for the coming night.

The wolf came down out of the foothills, running with the loose, fast-moving gait that consumed miles of hunting track. It was a big wolf, an old, grizzled *lobo* with massive jaws and huge, yellow fangs. It could run down a deer, even kill a cow, but it wasn't above picking up an easy meal.

Like the one it scented on the cooling air drifting up from the south where the bad-smelling lines that carried the worse-odoured beasts that howled too loud and spat fire went back and forth across the land.

The wolf's tongue hung out as it ran. It was hungry. It had been too long since it brought down the big prong-horn and the rumbling inside its belly said that even carrion would taste good.

It halted a respectful distance from the bodies, testing the night air with sensitive nostrils, scanning the moon-lit sand with implacable yellow eyes. It had never tasted human flesh before and still felt an inherent nervousness at the unfamiliar odours of metal and leather, and the curious scent of man flesh. It turned towards the horse, a warning growl rumbling throatily from between its salivating lips.

It trotted forwards and began to tear at the mustang's belly. The horse flesh tasted good.

The coyotes, scattered by the wolf's approach, slunk warily clear of the big, grey *lobo*. Less particular in their eating habits, they decided that it was safer to leave the more succulent meat to the wolf and make shift with the men. They spread out and began to gnaw at the bodies.

Azul felt a sudden sharp pain in his arm. He groaned, lifting his head.

A coyote snarled and darted back. Azul tried to shout, but his mouth was dry and seemed to be clogged with some sticky, salty substance. All that came out was a faint croak. The effort wasted him and his head slumped on to the sand. The coyote watched for a moment, then ran in again. Azul sensed it coming and concentrated on moving his right hand.

It was hideously difficult. He was only dimly aware of the Colt gripped tight in numb fingers, and he lacked the strength to raise the gun. He forced his thumb back against the hammer. It seemed to take an awfully long time and when he got it cocked he was no longer sure if he had the strength to squeeze the trigger.

The coyote fastened its jaws on his wrist. A second, emboldened, worried at his legs. A third drifted in, angling towards his stomach.

Azul thought about Nolan. He thought about his father. About his mother. He thought about the scalp Nolan had waved at him.

His finger clenched convulsively.

The Colt exploded sound across the night. Muzzle flash illuminated a snarling face, another that was bloody and bruised. The bullet hit a coyote, spinning it sideways with blood showing over its dusty pelt. Azul held the trigger down and thumbed the hammer again. The second shot blew sand over the corpse of Fox Runner. The coyotes and the wolf took off into the night.

Azul summoned the last vestiges of his waning strength to trigger a third shot. Then the darkness closed in again.

Something moved across his face. Something light and delicate, careful of waking him. He opened his eyes. The fly took off with an angry buzz.

For a while there was only blank brightness, but then his eyes found focus and he realised that he was staring at the sky. The sun was hot on his face and he knew that it must be just after noonday. He became aware of an emptiness in his hand and tried to lift himself to find the Colt.

Gentle hands pressed him down and he recognised the soft warmth of a blanket under his head. A woman's face hovered into view. It was a wide face, the eyes large and black above a broad nose and full-lipped mouth. Dark hair hung down from a blue bandanna that was tied about the crown of her head.

'Rest,' she murmured. 'You must rest.'

He tried to shake his head in disagreement. Tried to say that he had to get up and go after Nolan. But the effort was too much and he went back inside the warm red darkness of his mind.

The next time he woke it was dark and he smelled food cooking. He recognised the pungent odour of frying chiles and the sweeter smell of cornbread. Someone touched water to his lips and he gulped, suddenly knowing that he was thirsty.

'Easy. Rest.'

It was the same voice. An Apache voice. He opened his mouth to ask where he was, but an arm came round to cradle his head and a spoon was lifted to his mouth, dripping soup between his lips. He swallowed, grateful for the warmth of the food, for the strength it gave him.

Then the darkness came back again and he closed his eyes and slept.

The next time he stayed awake long enough to see that he was laid on a pine bed outside a hogan. There were children staring at him with wide, curious eyes. The woman appeared and shooed the children away. She fed him more soup and when two warriors approached, she shooed them away as she had done the children. The soup tasted good, but when he had drunk it all he found it too hard to speak and went back to sleep again.

When next he woke, the woman was waiting. She called the men over and they eased him up to a sitting position. The movement hurt him and he groaned. The woman smiled and lifted the spoon to his mouth. This time the soup was stronger, with tiny pieces of meat shredded into it. He was surprised to find he had an appetite.

'You will live,' said the woman. 'For a long time I thought that you might die. But now I think that you will live if you rest and let your body mend.'

'I cannot rest.' Azul looked around him. He was in an Apache *rancheria*, laid out on the couch where the sun could warm his body. 'I must find a man and kill him.'

'The one who did this to you.' The woman made a statement, not a question. 'You cannot kill him when you cannot stand. Rest and grow strong. Then kill him.'

Azul nodded, wondering why the soup made him so sleepy.

After that he stayed awake for longer periods and the soup got stronger and meatier, until he was chewing on large pieces that made his jaw ache and sent pain shooting up the left side of his face.

'Chew slowly,' said the woman. 'There are holes in your face where the pellets hit you. I have taken them all out and your face will heal, but take care.'

'Who are you?' asked Azul. 'Where am I?'

The woman smiled. 'I am called Dove Woman,' she said. 'I am a healer of the Chiricahua, your own people. We heard your shots and came to look. We found only you alive, so we brought you back to the *rancheria*.'

'The others?' Azul grunted. 'They are dead?'

'Three Ojo Caliente,' nodded Dove Woman. 'I recognised only Lame Pony. He was *bronco*: a bad Apache who made too much trouble.'

'He was a good friend to me,' murmured Azul. 'He gave his life up for me. I must find the man who killed him.'

'Not for a while,' smiled the healer, 'you are too badly hurt.'

'I thought I was dead,' said Azul; obstinately. 'That I live proves I must go after him.'

Dove Woman smiled again and pushed him back on to the couch. Azul was too weak to resist.

'Your face must heal,' she said. 'And your body. This

man you hunt used a shotgun: you are lucky it missed you. He also fired a pistol into your stomach, but his bullet hit the buckle on your belt. It cut you badly there and I had to sew the cuts. When you fell from the train you broke two ribs and damaged your left wrist. You were cut and bruised, but time will heal that.'

'I don't have time,' said Azul. 'I must go after him.'

'No,' said Dove Woman. 'You must rest until you are healed up and strong enough. If you go now you will die when your wounds open.'

Azul tried to lift his legs from the couch. They hurt when he moved them and he looked down. His waist was wrapped with bandages of cloth and rawhide, a loincloth fastened about his groin. Both legs were mottled with blue-black bruises that shaded into yellow at the edges. His left shoulder and most of the upper arm were wrapped in cloth and when he touched a hand to his face, he felt the gummy thickness of a poultice along his cheek and temple.

Dove Woman passed him a clay pot that held an aromatic liquid.

'Drink,' she said softly. 'It is a herb brew that will heal your body from the inside.'

Azul obeyed her. The drink induced a languor that made his eyes heavy, his voice slow. After a bit he went back to sleep.

The next day he asked Dove Woman how long he had been in the camp. 'Nineteen days,' she told him. 'You were unconscious for ten days while we fed you like a baby.'

'He will be gone,' moaned Azul. 'I must go after him.'

'A dead man does not ride far,' said the healer. 'The one you seek is alive, but you will die if you leave now.'

'I must find him,' Azul repeated. 'I swore an oath.'

'We know of your oath,' smiled Dove Woman. 'We know that Azul of the Chiricahua seeks vengeance for his parents and people. That is why we help you.' She handed him a plate of soft-fried meat and stewed vegetables. 'You hunt the man called Nolan. He rides with a Mexican called Raul Granos. My husband, Deer Killer, and two others trailed them to Fort Huachuca. From there they went down to Fronteras, then south. Others follow them now: you will know where they are.'

Azul thanked her and began to eat. If the warriors of this *rancheria* had taken the trouble to locate Nolan at all meant that they shared his purpose. Having accepted the undertaking, they would trail the dark man as far as was humanly – Apache – possible. They would ride in relays, taking spare mounts with them, alerting any wandering bands by means of smoke or mirror signals to pick up the trail. Azul had followed that same road in his youth, trailing Mexican border raiders deep into Sonora and Chihuahua without the quarry ever knowing of the men moving up behind them. It was the best possible scouting system he could wish for – far better than he hoped for – and he fell back into sleep feeling more comfortable than he had felt in days.

When they carried him out the next morning he insisted on getting to his feet. He was shaky and couldn't stand up for too long, but throughout the day he exercised his arms and wrists and hands, watched by the anxious children and a doubtful Dove Woman. He stood up twice more, each time walking a little farther. By sunset he was exhausted and ready to sleep, but he felt better than he had done in a long time.

And he knew that he would be leaving soon.

For the following week he forced himself to exercise, ignoring the pain, until he could move almost as lithely as before. His face and shoulder were healing up, leaving only a faint tracery of scars to mark the shotgun's blast. His ribs – so long as he kept them bound – gave him little trouble, and his wrist, although still stiff, was becoming usable again. His legs were the worst problem, but he bathed them and applied the herbal poultices Dove Woman provided to reduce the bruising and by the end of the week they were agile again.

Then Deer Killer came back. He had followed

Nolan's tracks down to Fronteras, then picked the man up south of the town. The trail had taken him as far as the Rio Aros, where a raiding party of Mimbreños and Chiricahua had agreed to delay their return to the Guadalupe Mountains and trail the two men south. The leader was known to Deer Killer, and had promised to send word once he was sure of Nolan's destination.

Thirteen more days passed before the word came in. Azul used them judiciously, working his body back to the peak of fitness smashed by his fall from the train. He could ride and shoot as well as ever, though he still found it necessary to nurse his left wrist and he doubted he could walk for too long. His face was almost healed, and his stomach gave him no trouble. He would carry a puckered, square-shaped scar for the rest of his life, and he still needed the bandages on his ribs. But hate spurred his recovery. That and Dove Woman's healing powers.

When the Mimbreño rider came into camp and told them Nolan was settled into Chihuahua, Azul said that he must leave.

Dove Woman gave him a package of herbs and poultices to apply to his wounds. Deer Killer gave him a pinto pony and a new Winchester. The whole village gave him a blessing.

He left at dawn, riding south and east on a line that would skirt the foothills of the Guadalupes and bring him out near the headwaters of the Bavispe. From there he would head over to the Casas Grandes and the Santa Maria, then hook past the Candlaerias in the direction of the Rio Conchos and the town of Chihuahua.

'Take care,' urged Dove Woman as he climbed astride the pinto. 'Be careful of your wounds.'

'I shall,' said Azul. 'But I intend to give wounds, not tend them.'

CHAPTER TEN

Tubac was due south of his position, around two days' ride away. Stopping off involved him in a slight detour from the most direct path to Chihuahua, but Azul wanted to see Carmady again. He felt he was owed an explanation.

When he reached the *pueblo* he went straight to Linda Velazquez's rooming house.

Linda was taking her mid-day meal in her private rooms. She looked surprised to see Azul come through the door.

'Where's Carmady?' he demanded. 'I want to talk to him.'

'*Querido!*' the woman smiled and stood up. 'We thought you were dead.'

'We?' Azul sat down, evading her arms. He helped himself to food.

'Carmady said you got killed.' She went back to the far side of the table, watching him. 'He got word from Tucson several days ago.'

'Where is he?' repeated Azul.

'He left.'

'When?'

Linda shrugged. 'Three days . . . maybe four.'

Azul helped himself to wine. 'You hiding him?'

Linda smiled: 'No. Why should I? Neither of you own me.'

'Sure,' said Azul. 'That's right. Out of sight is out of mind.'

The woman blushed; almost. 'I think he is going to Mexico,' she said. 'He heard that Nolan broke free with the help of a Mexican. He also heard that Nolan had sent a message to a man in Chihuahua. It was after that we heard you had been in Tucson. Then there was no word from you and we thought you must have died.'

'No,' said Azul softly. 'I didn't.'

He stood up and moved to the door.

Linda Velazquez rose to her feet and came round the table with a smile on her face.

'Stay with me,' she said. 'Let Carmady find Nolan.'

Azul swung the door open.

'Linda,' he said. 'I don't have the time. There'll be someone riding through soon enough. Your bed won't get too cold.'

Her face lost the smile. It got suddenly old and ugly with angry wrinkles.

'Bastardo!' she yelled. *'Bastardo lobo! Lobo loco!'*

Azul grinned and slammed the door in her face. He went out to the porch and mounted the pinto mustang. By the time the woman got out on to the street and began to shout after him he was trailing dust out of the town.

It took him a little over a week to get down to Chihuahua. The Bavispe was getting filled up with early snow from the Guadalupes and forced him to hunt around for a decent crossing place. Twice he hid from *Rurale* patrols, anxious to avoid direct confrontation with the Mexican authorities, and he skirted around the larger settlements like Fronteras and Casas Grandes. There were too many people there who might remember him and seek to delay him. He slept mostly in the open, keeping his legs close to the fire to ease the stiffness that seemed to grow with the long days in the saddle and the increasing cold. Autumn was beginning to show signs of the first fading into winter, and the nights up on the high plateau of northern Mexico were getting chilly enough to make him feel his hurts.

The day he reached Chihuahua was bright and sunny, warm with the languid heat that seems peculiar to Mexico. It was the kind of day a whiteman would ascribe to an Indian Summer.

Chihuahua stood out bright amongst the hills, sunlight reflecting off the flat roofs and corniches of the stucco buildings. A church bell dulled lazy sound over the town, and the streets looked quiet and sleepy. It was a large settlement, side streets radiating off the main thoroughfare with the buildings getting smaller as they got farther out. Off to one side was a spread of big houses, walled-in *haciendas* that had been around before the rest of the place got built. The kind of houses that looked run down and could still boast money.

Azul wondered where Nolan would be. He reined in and settled down to cook a meal: he planned to wait for night before going in.

Nolan was settled back against the cushions of a high wicker chair. He had a glass of whisky in his hand and a smile on his face that looked almost pleasant. His jacket was tossed over the chair beside him and he lounged in shirtsleeves and waistcoat. The shoulder rig holding his .38 Remington Star was buckled under his left arm, and he wore his Colt's Frontier model at his waist.

He was on the balcony of a nine-roomed *hacienda* a quarter mile from the centre of Chihuahua. He had bought the place with the stolen money because it made a good base and he fancied the idea of playing the leisured *yanqui* gentleman.

With Breed dead he could afford the luxury of taking a breath.

The house was surrounded by high brick walls plastered over with white clay. They were fourteen feet high all round the gardens, which ran out a thousand yards in each direction. There was a small gate cut into the east side, where the servants came in. Nolan had three servants. A cook; a housekeeper; and a general supervisor. The servants' gate was guarded by a man with a shotgun and two well-used Colts hung either side of his thickening waist.

The main gate was a fancy affair of intricately wrought iron with a massive lock and a second man with a shotgun guarding it. It opened on to a sand driveway that went up to the house. There was a third guard stationed at the door.

The door was made of solid oak with an interior cross-bar and a metal lock. The hinges were bolted into the filling of the walls, set inside a foot of solid adobe and stone. They opened into a huge room with polished pine floorboards and a big fireplace. A wide, wooden door opened off to the kitchen and a staircase of sculpted wood went up to the rooms above. There were four bedrooms, and two bathrooms with their own tubs. A small bell-tower was built on to the roof, its high-walled sides looking down on to the green slate of the lower storey, its height affording a view over the grounds.

There was a stable built up against the rear of the *hacienda*, and a small paddock for the horses. Under the place was a cellar.

The cellar covered most of the area beneath the foundations. It was cool and dark, the kerosene lanterns hung on the walls never quite managing to disperse the shadows. It was, nonetheless, a large, spacious area.

It was filled up with machinery.

At the centre of the ceiling there hung two rows of lanterns; when lit, they would throw light down on to the printing press located beneath. The press was several feet wide and more in length. An ink bucket stood at one end, with the attached equipment spaced down the cellar. There were two metal stamping plates on rollers at the end of the pressing table and buckets of acid and cleaning fluids all around. Big crates full of paper flanked the table, and on the side was a cutting jig. Two other tables looked like dress-makers equipment. They had treadles under the chairs and long loops of polished leather running up to a gantry bolted into the roof. The leather straps connected to the mechanisms of the cutters and the rollers.

The set-up had cost Nolan – and his partner – the

better part of five thousand dollars. Most of it spent on buying silence.

The house had cost another three. The guards and servants were bought off with higher wages than brooked questioning.

Nolan and Granos still had money to spend. On making money.

'When you gonna get it right?' asked Nolan. 'How long?'

Raul Granos shrugged and tried to smile.

'Soon,' he said. 'It's not so easy as you thought.'

He waited for Nolan's answer. He felt afraid as he waited: the dark man had that kind of effect on people.

'Why not?' Nolan emptied his glass and poured a fresh measure. He didn't offer Raul one. 'You're a printer, ain't you?'

'Yes,' said Raul. 'But I have never printed money before, so I must work carefully. It is a new technique: it requires a great deal of care. If we get it wrong we can only lose. We must print each bill exactly right, or it will be spotted.'

'An' maybe traced back,' grunted Nolan, reluctantly. 'How long before you get it right?'

Raul shrugged.

'A week?' he asked. 'Perhaps a little longer. The paper alone is difficult enough to match.'

'Yeah, I know. I heard it all before.' Nolan topped his glass. 'But meanwhile we're wastin' money that's gonna run out. The sooner you get that goddam press workin', the better. There ain't too many Americans buyin' places in Chihuahua, an' there's gonna be people lookin' fer us pretty damn' soon. When they start comin' in, we'll hafta to spend more to keep yore greaser friends oiled up an' talkin' in our favour. That's gonna cost us.'

Raul nodded and took the whisky bottle. He filled a glass up to the rim and downed it fast.

'*Claro*,' he said. 'We need to print a few bills. I understand that. But I still need the right ink and the right paper. That last consignment wasn't right.'

'Christ!' Nolan spat whisky over his pants. 'It cost enough. What was wrong?'

Raul topped his glass again, feeling nervous.

'It is a question of inking,' he said. 'The paper quality was good enough, but the ink was bad. It fouled the paper. If we are to do this thing right, we must have the proper paper to take the correct ink. Otherwise the notes will be spotted.'

'Christ!' grunted Nolan. 'I guess that means you want more money.'

Raul nodded. '*Si.* A thousand – maybe two – should do it. I must be careful where I buy, you understand?'

'I guess so,' said Nolan. 'Wait.'

He stood up and walked into the house. Raul had a room on the west side; Nolan's was on the east. He unlocked the door and closed it behind him. Then he knelt down and eased two boards up from the floor. They exposed a section of cross-timber and a wide gap. He hauled an oilskin sack out and tugged the draw-strings loose. The sack held money. He counted off two thousand dollars in fives, twenties, and ones. Then he wadded them all up in his hands and went back to the balcony.

He passed them to Raul after checking that the servants weren't watching. Raul thanked him and explained that he should go and meet a man who could find the right paper.

He was glad to get free of Nolan. The dark man made him nervous.

Nolan sat back and poured another whisky. It felt good, living the high life.

Carmady drank a beer up against the counter of the cantina called the *Vaquero Viejo.*

The beer was warm and watery, but it served to flush out the Pinkerton's mouth. He had drunk too much tequila that day, asking questions about the cold-eyed *norte americano* who had bought the old Ramez place and his Mexican *amigo*.

Carmady called for a second beer and tried to collect his thoughts, to equate them with his findings. He drank the second beer and called for a third, then decided to order a bottle of American whisky to clear his head.

He was pretty certain that the *norte americano* was Nolan. The description fitted and the set-up felt right. His informant in Chihuahua was sure that Raul Granos, a printer, had got word from a man in Tucson; had sold up his business on the strength of the message and ridden south. Raul Granos was a middle-aged Mexican given to wearing fancy clothes, all silver decorated. He had a knife scar on his right cheek.

The description fitted the man described by the depot official and passengers at Tucson.

Carmady had put two and two together and come up with a neat four.

Nolan had gotten away with money and printing plates. He wouldn't know how to use the plates, so he'd look for a man who could. Raul Granos was that man, and Nolan had sent for him. The Mexican had quit his place in Chihuahua and ridden up to Tucson to meet Nolan. Meanwhile, the American had shacked up with a whore while he waited. And the whore had run off with his money. Nolan had gone after her and killed her. Which got him arrested. Carmady had found that out when he visited Tucson. He couldn't persuade the sheriff to release Nolan into his custody, so he had taken a long chance and hired the half-breed he had heard about to do the job for him. That meant waiting around Tubac until he got word – one way or the other. He had figured that the 'breed was desperate enough to risk springing Nolan out of jail and kill him. That would have left Carmady to pick up the credit. And – if Azul had brought the plates and money back – with a tidy bank-roll. He hadn't counted on the half-breed getting himself killed. At least not while Nolan broke free.

That had spoiled his plans and prompted him to head fast for the one town he thought Nolan would head for: Chihuahua.

Now he had two options left open, both profitable in varying degrees.

One was to bring Nolan in, take all the credit along with the two thousand dollar reward.

The second was to find the scalphunter and talk a deal through, whereby John Michael Carmady got himself cut in as full partner on the printing deal.

There was a faint third, but he figured it too difficult to work. It would involve killing Nolan and taking the plates himself. But Nolan was an obviously difficult man to kill, and if he had a set-up working already it would be easier to cut in, rather than set up something new.

Carmady sipped his whisky and smiled. He felt confident of making money on this, whatever the outcome.

And that would be a pleasant change after the years of pounding boot leather and risking his life for the wages the Pinkerton organisation paid.

John Michael Carmady was forty-three years' old. He owned a frame house in Houston and four horses, one of them a half-blood Arab. He had exactly four hundred dollars and thirty cents in the bank of San Antonio, two good suits and three pistols. He had been married, but his wife left him when she got tired of wondering if he'd come home from a mission; and the Texas range wars were hotting up all the time. It was a lonely, miserable life for a range detective.

Carmady had volunteered for the Nolan thing when he got word that Harvey and Mitchell had been killed and the stolen money – and plates – had disappeared. He had used his contacts in Texas and New Mexico to open up a trail towards the man who had taken the stolen items. And the man who had sworn to kill him.

Along the way to Tucson and Tubac, the vague idea of cutting his losses had crystallised into a firm decision: he was going to grab a handful of heaven. He was going to take the money and run. Off into Mexico, or Europe; or wherever. He was going to give up worrying about some hired gunhawk shooting him in the back, or some frightened kid pulling a gun in a dirty Texas saloon and putting a slug into his belly. He was going to grab the money and run. Live easy. No cares. Just luxury all the way.

Now all he needed was to find Nolan and work it out.

He swallowed more whisky and smiled in anticipation. An American with money to spend couldn't be hard to find in a place like Chihuahua; it was just a question of waiting and working out the right approach.

He emptied his beer glass and called for a refill. When it came he asked about the whores the *cantina* had available. He thought he might as well enjoy himself.

Outside the *cantina* the sun got low in the sky and began to fade long shadows over the street. Up in the hills, a wolf howled. Carmady didn't hear the lonely sound: he had his face buried in the hair of a *puta* called Rosita and was too busy congratulating himself to hear anything. Or see the bored expression on Rosita's face as she picked her nose and faked grunts of ultimate pleasure while she waited for the *yanqui* to spend his two dollars' worth and leave her alone.

Azul heard the sound and wondered if it was an omen.

When the wolf howls a man watches . . . Old Sees-The-Fox had told him that. Mostly, it seemed to mean that the wolf knew where the game was, or when danger threatened. But Sees-Both-Ways had been a shaman of the Chiricahua, and he had set a different interpretation on animal sounds.

The dead are lonely and sometimes enter animals to make themselves heard. Azul recalled the teachings of his Apache childhood. *The whitemen say that when the son of their God died a cock crowed three times. Perhaps his soul went into the bird. Perhaps there was nothing bigger it could enter. Listen to the sounds in the night because they can tell you things you will not hear while the sun is high, and the wise warrior listens to all the sounds. Both loud and small.*

Azul listened to the wolf.

He kicked sand over his fire and climbed back on the pinto mustang.

The pad saddle felt good after months of riding the *pinda-lick-oyi* leather.

The wolf howled again.

Azul heeled the mustang up to a canter that took them fast towards the lights of Chihuahua.

As he entered the sprawl of huts trailing out past mainstreet, the wolf howled a third time. The half-breed smiled and wondered if the animal knew more than men guessed.

Maybe he would kill a deer when his business was done, and leave it in the hills for the wolf to eat. A thanks-offering.

CHAPTER ELEVEN

Azul rode slowly up mainstreet, hoping that no one would recognise him. If there were warrants out in Galenas and Fronteras, it was possible that word had spread this far south, too. He chose, however, to take a chance on the Mexican authorities confining their searching to the two towns he was known to have visited and the border. As an Apache, he had often ridden down as far as Chihuahua, but as Matthew Gunn – as Breed – he was notorious mostly around the border country. In any event, he was determined to locate Nolan – irrespective of legal hindrance.

He settled his stetson over his face and eased the pinto up the road.

Mainstreet was, in effect, a huge plaza. Like most large Mexican towns, Chihuahua was set out around the central hub of city life. There was a tiled boulevard, the *rambla*, set with palmetto and jacaranda trees running up the centre of the street. Traffic was eased out on to the sand roadways skirting the *rambla*, and busy waiters dodged amongst the horses and the wagons to carry drinks and food to the customers settled around the wood tables on the plaza. There was a constant flow of people moving clockwise around the square and a counter flow strolling in the opposite direction. The outer ring was composed mostly of families, parents walking with daughters or grandmothers, carrying babies, talking, staring.

The inner ring was composed mostly of young men in groups of three and four. They were dressed up in fancy outfits all silvery with conchos and overworked gunbelts, and they grinned and chuckled as they caught the eye of the girl they fancied. When they caught the grim gaze of the accompanying father they got confused and hurried on, so that the central movement was brisker than the stately progress of the outer circle.

It was the Mexican custom of the *pasear*: the evening stroll at which the young men snatched a hurried word with their sweethearts, and the whole town showed off its finery and caught up on local gossip.

At the far end of the *rambla* there was a big fountain with a statue of Pizarro built up above the spilling water. The water ran lazily down from a big basin with gutters cut along the sides to take it off under the street where it probably supplied water to the gardens of the richer houses. There was a bar to the right of the fountain and a second to the left.

Azul reined in and went inside the place on the left.

There was a hitching rail dug into the side street with four horses tied up. Azul left the pinto alongside.

The bar was low-roofed and bright with light. It was packed with vaqueros and storekeepers, and smelled different to an American saloon. Azul pushed up to the bar and called for tequila. The *patrón* gave him a curious glance, then shrugged as though dismissing his doubts and opened a bottle. He reached behind the counter to lift a clay cup and set it down in front of the half-breed.

'Gracias,' murmured Azul, dropping a coin on to the rough pine.

'De nada.' The man picked up the coin and bit it. It was a five dollar piece. He dropped it into the leather pouch hung off his belt. 'I must find some change.'

'Don't bother,' said Azul. 'Pay me with words.'

'I am no writer,' grunted the Mexican. 'I run a clean bar, not dabble with stupid scribbling.'

Azul smiled. 'But you see people. And a man as important as the owner of so fine a *cantina* must know who lives in this splendid city.'

The Mexican puffed up, hiking his shoulders back and straightening his spine so that his eyes got level with Azul's nose.

'Of course,' he said. 'Ramon Garcia knows everyone. Who are you looking for?'

'An American,' smiled Azul. 'A tall man with dark hair and green eyes. He favours black clothes. He might be accompanied by a Mexican.'

'Ah!' Garcia tugged at his moustache. 'There are two Americans in town. One of them is a man such as you describe. Word has it that he carries money with him. At least, he purchased the old *hacienda* and has since hired servants, and *pistoleros* to guard it for him. He has an *amigo mexicano*, a man called Raul Granos. Poor Raul.'

'Why poor?' Azul filled his glass and extended the bottle in invitation. 'With a rich *yanqui amigo*, he cannot be too badly off.'

Garcia found an empty pot and let Azul fill it. 'Raul sold his business,' he said. 'He had a nice little business as a printer. He printed our paper and when we wanted to make bills for advertising, or weddings . . . you know the kind of thing . . . Raul was the man we went to. Then he closed down and rode north. He came back with his tail between his legs and his *yanqui* friend to pay his bills.'

'And his friend,' said Azul, 'is a tall American with dark hair and green eyes?'

Garcia nodded. The movement set his jowls to wobbling.

'*Si,*' he said, shaking a limp wrist in an obscene gesture. 'I think that maybe Raul has chosen the back trails . . . '

'Where do they live?' Azul interrupted Garcia and made up for it by filling his pot again. 'Do you know?'

'The *hacienda* is just the other side of town,' said the barkeeper. 'A walled place with men to guard the gates. I think they have something to hide.'

His dark, red-veined eyes got bright and piggy.

'Are you with them?'

'Is that likely?' said Azul. 'The American owes me a debt I wish to collect. He is unwilling to pay it, so I must find him and claim it.'

Garcia smiled as though he enjoyed the thought. 'The place is about a quarter a mile out. If you were to take the road opposite this *cantina* and ride as far as the broken pine on the side of the road you would find the house a little way up along the street facing the tree.'

'Thank you,' said Azul. 'It is pleasant to meet a honest man.'

He set down his glass and turned away. He hadn't thought to find Nolan so easily, but it had to be the scalphunter. He walked out through the bead curtain covering the doorway and reached down to loose the pinto from the hitching rail.

Something hard and cold dug in his back as his hand touched the single rein.

A hard, cold voice said: 'Don't turn round. Just put

your hands on the rail. Don't move, or three guns will kill you.'

Azul put his hands on the rail. The hard thing went on sticking into his back, but the voice moved round in front and got a face. It was a cold face with a black moustache dribbling over the lips and hard grey eyes glistening from under a grey, peaked cap. A *Federale* cap. Under the face was a uniform. A grey uniform with a black Sam Browne spread neatly over the chest and waist. On the right hip there was a big holster with the flap open. The gun that would usually be inside the holster was out and lifted up into his face. It was a Smith & Wesson American .44 calibre. The hammer was all the way back. Azul could see the tension in the trigger finger even through the leather of the black glove the lieutenant was wearing.

'What in the hell is this?' he said. 'What have I done?'

'A great deal,' said the lieutenant. 'The killing of Ramon Padillo for one thing. Then there was Amos Grieve in Fronteras. I believe, too, that some *yanqui* lawmen would welcome talking with you. There is a considerable amount of money available to the man who captures Breed.'

Two *Federale* troopers came out from the shadows. They both carried Winchesters. Both rifles were levelled steady on Azul's ribs. The third stayed hard and fast on his back.

'I done nothing in Chihuahua,' he said. 'How come you're taking me?'

'Money,' said the lieutenant. 'There is a reward of six hundred and fifty dollars American posted on your capture. The authorities in Texas and Nevada offer more.'

Azul felt a hand move in and lift the Colt from his holster. To his left, the Bowie knife was lifted. They forgot the throwing knife tucked down into his boot.

'How come you recognised me?' he asked. 'I didn't think there'd be posters this far south.'

The officer laughed: 'We were warned. We had word.'

'From who?' Azul's face got pale with anger. 'Who told you?'

A rifle moved up in obeyance of the lieutenant's gesture and struck the underside of his chin. Azul lifted back from the rail. His legs hit the boardwalk and he sat down. The two troopers flanking him moved round to stick their Winchesters tight into his ribs. The probing muzzles hurt him and he loosed an unwilling groan.

'A man called Carmady,' said the officer. 'He told us. Now stand up. It will take a few days to get word from Fronteras, but when it arrives we shall hang you. Like the *lobo* dog you are.'

Azul stood up. The two troopers fell into step behind him, their rifles touching his back enough to remind him of their presence. The lieutenant walked alongside, on the right, with his S & W angled past his trim belly to level on the half-breed. The third soldier followed on with the pinto mustang in tow.

They took him all the way down the *rambla* to the *Federale* station and threw him into a cell. It was a small cell with wet stone walls on three sides and a wood door filling up most of the fourth. The door had a metal grille set into the middle, at head height. Facing the grille was a window. It was barred with steel shafts an inch thick apiece. There were four bars over ten inches of window: very little light would ever come into the cell. The floor was paved stone, covered with rushes and sand that held thick memories of bygone occupants. There was a straw mattress on the floor by the northern wall. It had holes in it and yellow stains. There was a bucket that had once held fresh water. Now it looked like the spillings from the fountain in the square. The air smelled hot and damp; it smelled of urine and sweat and lost hopes. There was no light, and the window faced a side street with high buildings.

It was a lost and lonely place. The kind of place a man dreams about when he dreams of death.

Azul kicked the mattress. Bugs ran from the cracks. He turned it over. The underside was liquid with damp and thick with insects.

He went over to the corner of the cell and squatted down. Bracing his back against the wall, he hunkered into a crouch and dropped his head over his folded arms. He closed his eyes and did his best to sleep while he was still thinking; working out his position, his situation.

He still had the throwing knife inside his right moccasin, and no one had thought to check his vest. There were six cartridges in the lower right pocket. Six .45 shells that might prove useful. Given the right opportunity.

John Michael Carmady congratulated himself on his powers of observance and the speed with which he put them into effective operation.

It had been pure luck to spot Azul – Breed – lounging up to the bar as he left Rosita's room. But it had taken, so Carmady told himself, real skill to recognise the situation and make capital out of it before the half-breed could even know what was happening.

He had snuck back into the shack and climbed out through a window. Then he had run to the *Federale* station and warned Lieutenant Guerra of the sadistic killer boasting his presence in a peaceful town like Chihuahua. The Pinkerton badge had convinced the lieutenant of Carmady's honest intentions, and mention of the rewards – which, of course, Carmady would forfeit in the interests of justice – had gone a long way to getting Guerra on his feet and working.

Carmady had watched Guerra take his three-man squad off to arrest Azul, then run back down the plaza to be sure the *Federales* were locking him up.

Convinced of that, he decided to ride out and tell Nolan of his coup. And put his proposition to the owner of the printing plates.

The welcome was less than he had hoped for.

Getting the address of the *hacienda* had cost him ten dollars in bribes and tequila. The ride out, for all that it was short, was rocky with the effects of too much liquor. Then he had spent a long time arguing with the guard before he even got into the place.

Then Nolan got tough.

'Why should I cut you in?' he asked. 'You got no authority down here. That goddam Pinkerton badge don't mean a single damn' thing south o' the border.'

'Means a whole on the north side, though.' Carmady tried not to slur his words: he wanted to put up a good impression. 'I got contacts in Texas and New Mexico that could ease the money through real easy. Like feedin' milk to a baby. I got a Pinkerton badge to back me up, an' that's a whole lotta authority. I could tell them I killed you an' the plates an' money got lost.'

'I could just print it up an' bank it,' said Nolan. 'Why should I cut you in?'

'Insurance,' said Carmady. 'I'm an upstanding citizen who won't get questioned when I start puttin' those bills in my bank. All them nice five dollar bills you got set to print.'

'You're pretty sure of yoreself,' said Nolan. 'You took a long chance comin' here. Why shouldn't I just kill you an' get done with it?'

Carmady smiled. 'You killed two Pinkertons already,' he said. 'That's what got me on your trail. Kill another, an' the whole organisation will be after you.'

Nolan nodded. 'All right, he murmured, 'it makes sense. I'll cut you in.'

'Good,' said Carmady. 'How about showin' me the set-up?'

Nolan stood up and led the way down to the basement. Carmady followed on behind, deciding not to tell about Azul, locked up in the local jail: it was a trump card to hold in hand.

He followed Nolan all the way down to the cellar, taking the precaution of easing the Merwin & Hulbert pocket gun clear of his shoulder-holster and settling it down inside his right-hand hip pocket.

Nolan swung the cellar doors shut and gestured at the machinery.

'I guess you know about the plates,' he said. 'They should be working soon. At least that's what Raul says, an' he's the printer. It seems we need some kinda special paper, which should be in pretty soon.'

Carmady walked around the printing press.

'Jesus!' he said. 'You sure laid out a whole lotta money to set this up.'

'Yeah,' said Nolan. 'I did. More than I'm willin' to share with some hasbeen sonofabitch Pinkerton.'

Carmady jerked back, recognising the menace in Nolan's voice.

He was too late: the dark man stepped up behind him and swung the Colt's Frontier up out of the holster and down.

Nolan didn't fire the pistol. He drew and reversed the gun, switching it round so that the butt crashed solidly on to the back of Carmady's neck. The Pinkerton groaned and slumped forwards, fighting the numbing pain that threatened to freeze his arms. He tried to draw the Merwin & Hulbert from his pocket, but Nolan grabbed his wrist and twisted it up behind his back. The Colt hammered a second time against Carmady's neck.

Nolan eased a foot forwards to kick the Pinkerton's legs out from under his body. The man was badly stunned, and the movement came easy. Carmady slumped like a soggy bag.

'Bastard!' Nolan snarled. 'You want a share? All right, bastard, I'll give you a taste of it.'

He shoved the Colt back inside the holster and slammed his hand down on to the back of Carmady's skull. The Pinkerton groaned again as his throat hit the edge of the big bucket. Nolan hiked his arms up so that they dangled over the rim. Then he stooped down to lift the man's legs.

He tilted Carmady up and over, shoving him face down into the vat.

Carmady screamed once as his face hit the acid and began to burn. Then his own body weight carried him under and all Nolan had to do was feed the kicking limbs down into the seething liquid.

The acid ate into cloth and skin. It dissolved flesh from bone with horrible speed. The cheap cloth of Carmady's suit disappeared as though washed away, followed by his flesh. Much sooner than Nolan had thought there was only a skeleton left to mark the dreams of a dissatisfied Pinkerton. All that was left to mark the place of John Michael Carmady was a grinning skull with empty sockets where the eyes had been and shredding trailers of cloth bubbling up around the bones.

Nolan used the long tweezers Raul Granos had bought to lift metal safely clear of the acid vat to fish Carmady's remains clear of the bucket. He pulled on a pair of leather gloves and spread a sheet of oilskin on the floor of the cellar.

When he had all the bones and flesh and remnants of cloth clear of the vat he folded the sheet of oilskin and tied it with waxed twine. Then he took it out behind the house and dumped it under a jacaranda at the far end of the spread. He walked back and got a spade, then dug a grave about two feet deep. He kicked what was left of Carmady into the hole and filled it up. After that he stamped the earth down flat and kicked leaves and fallen flowers over the hole. Then he went back to the house and wiped the spade clean on a rag that he tossed into the acid bucket.

All that was left of John Michael Carmady was a brass badge and a pistol. Those Nolan hid alongside the money, under the boards flooring his room.

After that, the dark man went out on to the balcony of his *hacienda* and poured himself a whisky.

He felt very safe, insured by money and a firm knowledge of his own skill with a gun or an awkward situation. There was nothing left, now, to spoil his plans, and once Raul had printed up a reasonable amount of five dollar bills and taught him to use the machinery, he could get rid of the Mexican.

And then, with Breed dead, he could enjoy life without troubles or cares.

Nolan emptied his glass and shouted for the servants to bring him food.

CHAPTER TWELVE

Azul passed the night thinking and sleeping.

He guessed that Carmady must have been the one to inform the *Federales* of his presence – which had to mean the Pinkerton wanted him out of the way. The only reason he could think of for the agent to double-cross him like that was that Carmady wanted a cut of Nolan's loot, and was afraid that Azul might foul up his deal. It was the only reasonable theory. And it meant that Nolan would most likely hear about him before the night was out.

Furiously, Azul tried to find a means of escape.

The bars at the window were solid. Even with the use of his throwing knife it would take days to chip one loose, let alone the several that would be necessary to open a gap wide enough for him to wriggle clear. Walls and floor and ceiling were, if anything, more solid still. The door was inches thick with the hinges on the outside and one of those huge Mexican locks. The bars in the peep-hole were carefully spaced: too close together for a prisoner to get a hand through.

That left two possible exits.

He could try to down a guard and fight his way from the *Federale* station. Or he could wait until they took him out to hang him and try then.

Both chances seemed slim.

He doubted the latter would be workable. His wrists would be tied when they took him out, and there would be a crowd come to watch him die. He decided to make an attempt to break out.

When he heard the soldiers moving about he slid the throwing knife from his moccasin and cradled the slender blade in his right hand, hidden between his arm and his body. After a while he heard bolts slide back and a key turn noisily in the lock. The door swung open. Azul tensed, standing back against the corner of the cell.

The muzzle of a Winchester angled round the door-frame, followed by a trooper with a smile on his face and a second armed soldier close behind him.

'Breakfast, *indio*,' said the Mexican. 'You stand back there where we can see you.'

A third trooper appeared, carrying a bowl. He set it down on the floor, just inside the door.

Azul weighed the odds: they looked bad. Both rifles were cocked and pointed straight at him. The third man was nervous enough to bolt at the slightest movement. He stayed motionless, watching the Mexicans back out. Watching the door close. Listening to the sound of the lock turning and the bolts slamming back home.

He sidled round to the door and pushed the knife back inside his moccasin. He needed some other plan if he was to get free and kill Nolan.

He thought about it as he checked his breakfast. The bowl contained coffee and a chunk of hard, stale bread. The coffee tasted sour and long-brewed; the bread was tough enough to break teeth. He drank the coffee and gnawed the bread. Then he settled back on the bug-infested mattress and thought some more.

At noon they brought him a dish of foul-tasting stew. It was mostly water with tiny pieces of gristle floating amongst the curled and aged remnants of the vegetables. He drank it all.

Just after sunset they fed him again. This time he got a piece of slightly fresher bread and tin mug of watery coffee.

'You're lucky,' remarked one of the *Federales*. 'You get fed better than most.'

'Why?' asked Azul.

'You have money.' The trooper shrugged. 'The others get only the slops.'

Azul remembered the coins he had carried on the pinto mustang. He had forgotten them, because money had never meant very much to him and he had thought that Nolan had taken it all along with the black horse. All except for the few coins on his person – the coins the *Federales* were using to buy his food.

'Can I have more coffee then?' he asked. 'A decent cupful in a mug that doesn't leak?'

'Sure.' The soldier grinned. 'It can be arranged. It will cost you another dollar.'

Azul shrugged. 'I may as well enjoy myself. I can't spend it after you hang me.'

'That's true,' said the man. 'But it means trouble for us. We have to go out and get it for you.'

Azul grinned. 'Why not buy a couple of bottles of mescal, too? One for me, to ease me through the hours of waiting. And a second for yourselves? To show my gratitude for your trouble.'

The *Federale* grinned. 'Sure. You are most generous. If the money were left, the *teniente* would grab it all for himself.'

'Then hurry,' said Azul. 'Get both bottles before he comes back.'

The door swung shut on three smiling faces. Azul squatted down and dunked the bread in the coffee: it made the crust taste better. He chewed slowly between sips of the tepid liquid, an idea taking shape inside his mind.

It was full dark by the time the coffee arrived. The

same three troopers brought it, in a shiny tin mug with the stamp of a Mexico City company on the handle. They brought an old whisky bottle, too, filled with home-brew mescal, and a cheap clay pot. They shut the door behind them and left Azul to enjoy himself.

He drank the coffee. It tasted good after the dregs he had been served, but the mug interested him far more. He took it over to the mattress and studied it as best he could in the faint light from the building across the alley.

When he was satisfied that the mug was built solid he pulled out his knife and set to punching a hole through the base. The tin was cheaply made and thin enough to puncture. He worked a hole through, using the knife like a drill, then set it aside.

He tasted the mescal. The liquor was rough and fiery, burning his mouth. He swallowed, and felt flame burn in his belly. He smiled, and put the bottle carefully down against the nearest wall.

He emptied his pockets. The six shells he knew about, and two more he had forgotten, were set out on the driest part of the mattress. He used the knife to prise the lead slugs loose from the cartridges, then poured the black powder into the coffee mug. He eased the detonation caps out of the brass bases and gentled them down into the powder. The whole assemblage occupied only about half the mug. He spread his bandanna out and tipped the mess of powder and fulminate caps over the cloth. Then he grasped the mug between interlocked fingers and began to squeeze. The tin was harder to crumple than he had thought, but after a hard time crushing he got the rim shoved inwards, reducing the capacity to a fraction of its original size.

He picked up a fulminate cap and dropped it into the cup. Using his knife, he eased it over the hole and tucked it down. Then he used his bandanna as a filter to pour the mess of powder and caps into the mug. He wadded it all tight with straw and cut the bandanna into strips.

Using the cloth, he lashed the mug against the door's lock, fixing the open end as close as he could to the hole. Then he soaked a few strips of the bandanna in mescal and tied them around the mug, leaving them trailing down over the plugged hole with the fulminate cap.

He soaked another length of the cloth in mescal and set it on the window shelf. It was the driest place in the whole cell. He lifted the knife and struck it against the stonework. Sparks glittered and died. He rasped the knife down again, ignoring the tiny burnings that spattered his arms and hands. A third time, then a fourth. Then the sparks hit the mescal-soaked cloth and took a hold.

The mescal flared up, igniting the cloth. Azul lowered a second strip, slowly, into the flame. It caught, and he dropped a section over the sill as he turned to the wall.

He picked up the near-full bottle and poured the contents over the mattress. He dragged the stinking cloth over to the door, lifting it up so that if the door should open, it would fall outwards.

Then he darted back to the window shelf and grabbed the strip of burning cloth.

He threw it on to the mattress.

For a moment the cloth burned fitfully and he began to lose hope. Then a little tongue of flame licked out, sputtering in the damp air. It drew itself up into a tall, blue-yellow ghost that danced over the mattress. Abruptly, the tiny tongue became a great wave of flame that washed over the mattress like surf surging across a beach.

The flames reached up to lick against the door and the ceiling. The damp stone seethed, giving off steam. Condensation dripped down on to the burning straw, damping it so that it smouldered and the flames died. In their place came great gouting billows of black smoke as the fire fought the moisture and hurried trails of bugs ran from the burning material.

The flame reached up to the cloth wrapped around the mug. Lit it.

The trailers of cloth blazed.

There was a brighter spurt of flame as the fulminate was ignited by the heat.

Then a sudden, sharp explosion as the powder inside the tied-down mug went off.

Light blasted out into the dim corridor of the jail. It blasted back into the cell. Azul hurled forwards against the door.

He held the throwing knife in his right hand, the empty mescal bottle in his left. The door gave, leaning out as *Federales* began to shout and the outer doors began to open.

Azul stepped back. Took another run. He hit the door with his left shoulder. It sprang open. Smoke billowed into the corridor. Azul felt flame in his hair, pain in his arm and hurt ribs.

He dropped to his knees, hefting the throwing knife back.

A trooper showed up the corridor. He held a pistol in his left hand. He began to cough as the smoke ran up towards the fresher air. Azul's arm lifted over and down. The knife spun from his fingers like a glittering bolt. It caught the *Federale* in the throat, choking off his cough inside the flow of blood from his adam's apple.

Azul ran forwards. He threw the mescal bottle past the door and stooped down to jerk the knife from the man's throat. He tugged it sideways, slicing through windpipe and arteries and veins, leaving the soldier choking out his life in a great spill of crimson blood. At the same time, he lifted the gun. It was a Colt's .45 Cavalry model. He cocked the hammer as he went through the door.

There were three steps up into the outer office. He took them at a run with bullets hitting stone over his head. He powered across the threshold, firing at the first man he saw. A *Federale* went down with blood spilling out over his dirty uniform. He clutched his stomach and doubled over, trying hard to scream through the blood coming out of his mouth.

There were three more there.

Azul shot one as he rolled. His bullet went in just above the man's holster. It spun him round as flesh gouted from his hip and his leg gave way. The soldier dropped the Winchester he was firing and began to scream and crawl away.

Azul rolled, still firing, and fetched up behind a desk. One man went down with his face blown away, groaning as he tried to claw the pain clear of his missing eyes and shattered nose. His hands gave up the effort and dropped away. He slumped back against the far wall and bled over the floor.

The third *Federale* poured five bullets into the desk. They blew an inkwall apart, shattered a row of pens, ploughed two long furrows down the woodwork, and broke the key sticking out of a drawer. Azul's fourth shot caught him high on the right side of his chest. It went through the pectoral muscles and deflected off the clavicle into a lung. The *Federale* was hurled back against the wall. He left a great scarlet smear down the paintwork as he slumped to the floor.

Azul twisted and squeezed off a shot at the man crawling towards the door.

It caught the Mexican in the side of his face, entering at the back of his gaping jaw and ricochetting off the bone to drive up through the roof of his mouth into his brain. It came out in a sticky fountain of hair and bone, intermingled with blood and brain tissue. The *Federale* jerked, stretching his arms forwards as though they were drawn out on wires. His hands spread wide and his legs straightened. He hit the floor with a dull, soggy sound and lay still.

Azul dropped the Colt and climbed to his feet. He found his own gun in the lowest drawer of the desk. It was tucked away with his belt wound round it, the Bowie knife still in the sheath. He pulled the belt out and slid the drawer closed.

As he stood up, the outer door opened and Lieutenant Guerra walked through.

The *teniente* looked dusty and irritable. He was slapping gauntlets against his coat, and coughing as the dust rose up and watered his eyes. The coat was a long, yellowish duster that whirled its tails over the head-shot *Federale* before Guerra realised the corpse was there.

When he looked down, he dropped his gloves and began to reach inside his coat as he stared around the room.

Azul was behind the desk. He had his gunbelt in his left hand, the throwing knife in the right. Guerra was carrying the S & W American on his right hip with the flap of his regulation holster buttoned down. Azul grinned: it was no contest.

He flipped the knife underhand, aiming with the precision of long practice.

The blade caught Guerra in the fleshy part of his right arm, the force of it twisting his arm out away from his gun. Azul powered across the table as the lieutenant staggered back, swinging the gunbelt in a short, vicious arc.

The holster, with the full weight of the Colt behind it, slammed into Guerra's face. It snapped his head to the side so that he grunted and fell against the door. Azul swung the belt back, slapping the holster against the other side of Guerra's glaze-eyed face. The *Federale* officer buckled at the knees, folding forwards. Azul swung a shoulder under the deadweight, hefting the lieutenant up on his back and carrying him across the room to the desk. He set the man down in the chair and slapped his face. It was almost an afterthought to tug the knife free of his arm.

Guerra woke up with the pain.

'*Bastardo lobo,*' he moaned. 'You will pay for this.'

'Shut up!' Azul snapped the gunbelt around his waist and tucked the throwing knife back inside his moccasin. 'Listen to me.' He drew the Colt and thumbed the hammer close enough to Guerra's ear for the lieutenant to wince at the sound of the triple click. 'There will be people coming to find out what the noise was. When they come I shall let you stand up and go over to the door to explain. I shall be close to you with my gun pointed at you. Give them some excuse and don't let anyone come in here. Send them all away fast. Otherwise I shall kill you.'

Guerra moaned and nodded and rubbed at his bleeding arm. The cloth of his duster was stained brown with blood, and both his cheeks were bluish-yellow where the gunbelt had landed. His right eye was puffy and red, a heavy bruise forming along the line of the cheekbone.

Footsteps dinned outside and the door began to open.

'Stand up,' snarled Azul, 'and remember what I said.'

Guerra stood up. The door opened. The lieutenant stepped out from behind the desk. Azul moved over to the curtained window, standing inside the swing of the door, so that he was hidden from view.

'Que va?' said a voice he didn't know. 'What's going on?'

He held the Colt at waist height, rock-steady on Guerra's belly.

'Nothing,' said the *Federale* lieutenant. 'A prisoner tried to break loose, that's all.'

He stepped round to block the door, placing his body so that it hid the corpses. He smiled with one eye on Azul's gun.

'But all that firing.' The speaker sounded unconvinced. 'We heard shots. People screaming.'

Guerra smiled and shrugged. 'Someone got a pistol to the half-breed,' he said. 'He tried to break out, but we killed him.'

He raised a hand to touch his cheek, wincing at the livid bruise.

'He almost made it, but we kept him back inside. There's nothing to worry about: go on home.'

Reluctantly, the footsteps went away and Guerra closed the door.

'Lock it,' grunted Azul. 'Then back up against the wall.'

Guerra locked the door and stepped backwards. He came close to falling over the body of the trooper closest to the door and grimaced in distaste as he saw that he was standing in a puddle of blood and brain mush. Azul went over to him and tugged the S & W clear of the flapped holster. It was an unfamiliar pistol and it took him a few moments to work out that the chamber broke open on a hinge screw where the underpinning of the barrel joined the frame. When he thumbed the catch, the whole thing snapped apart and spat cartridges into the air. Azul kicked them aside and tossed the gun across the room.

'Where's my horse?' he said.

Guerra swallowed hard. 'Out back,' he said. 'In the corral with ours.'

'Anyone there?' asked Azul.

Guerra shook his head.

'Good,' said Azul. 'I hope you're not lying. If you are, I'll kill you first. Show me the way.'

Guerra moved off past the bodies towards the cell block. Azul called for him to halt at the door and stepped back to lift a Winchester off of the mounting rack. The carbine was a late model, and loaded. Azul dropped his Colt into the holster and levered a shell into the Winchester's breech. Then he reached back and swept the lantern hung behind the desk off its hook. The glass funnel shattered and spread kerosene over the floor. Azul reached up to lift the centre light from its hook and tossed it into the blaze. There was the stifling smell of burning hair and a cartridge exploded as he shoved Guerra down the cell block.

The other cells were empty and the mattress had stopped burning, leaving only the thick, nauseating odour of smouldered straw and heated urine. Smoke hung in dank, black streamers along the floor, gusting forwards as the fire in the outer office took hold and created a draught.

Guerra led the way past Azul's cell to a tiny door at the end of the building. He produced a key and hurried through, coughing loudly until Azul shoved the Winchester into his back and told him to keep quiet.

The lieutenant had lied about the horses: there was a sleepy-eyed trooper fumbling his way out of a barn on the far side of the yard. The man was too far away, and too far lost in sleep to have heard the excitement. But he was awake now. Azul shot him in the chest. He pitched back into the stable.

Azul shoved Guerra onwards and went inside the barn. There was a double row of stalls holding the *Federale* horses, and one of them contained the pinto.

'Saddle up,' grunted Azul, pushing Guerra down the aisle. 'We're takin' a ride.'

The lieutenant buckled a high-cantled saddle on to a big grey stallion, then put Azul's pad saddle over the pinto. The horses could smell the smoke by now and were getting skitterish. Guerra opened the stalls on Azul's order and waited until the half-breed was mounted before climbing astride his own horse. There was shouting from inside the *Federale* station.

Azul shouted for Guerra to open the other stalls, then whooped the nervous horses clear. They spilled out like childen let early from school, skirling round the corral as men came running out of the rear door. Azul grabbed the left-side rein on Guerra's horse and went out past the stampeding animals.

There was a low fence built up against the adobe walls at the rear of the station. He headed the pinto mustang straight at it, laughing as the pony flew high over the rails. Guerra's grey took the fence like a contemptuous bird and thundered down the alley behind the pinto.

Azul went out to the north side of town and rode a clear five miles before halting. The mustang – Apache-bred – was willing to go on running, but the grey stallion was winded, panting as heavily as its rider. Azul reined in and climbed down. He ground-hitched the pinto and went over to Guerra with the Winchester canted up at the man's chest. Guerra was slumped down in the saddle, both hands clasped tight over the horn. There was blood running through the fingers of his right hand.

Azul hauled him down and stretched him on the ground. He pulled the duster clear of Guerra's shoulder and stripped off the uniform. Guerra's shirt was bloody from bicep to wrist, the knife wound refusing to close up under the pounding of the ride. Azul used the lieutenant's shirt to bandage the wound: there were sound reasons for keeping him alive.

He finished his primitive doctoring and slapped Guerra back to consciousness.

'Listen,' he said. 'I want you to understand exactly what I say. If you don't and you do something wrong – anything at all – I shall kill you. Do you understand?'

Guerra moaned and nodded.

'There is a man called Nolan,' said Azul. 'You are going to take me to him. You know where he lives?'

'The big house,' grumbled Guerra. 'The old Ramez place.'

'Take me there,' said Azul. 'When we get to the gates you must get me in. I hear he has guards.'

'He does.' Guerra sat up and clutched at his arm. He seemed surprised to find it dressed. Azul pulled the jacket around his shoulders. 'He has a man on both gates and one on the door.'

'Who else?' Azul fastened the jacket and draped the duster over Guerra's shoulders. 'How many more?'

'Raul Granos stays there. There are a few servants . . . a cook, a maid, someone else. No more than three.'

Guerra huddled down inside the coat, seeming to take comfort from its warmth. 'Why do you help me? Why not kill me?'

'You're too useful,' grunted Azul. 'Listen: you must take me to Nolan and get me inside the place. Maybe then I'll let you live.'

He dragged Guerra up on his feet and got him on to

the stallion. He mounted the pinto and rode off after the *teniente* with the Winchester canted over his hips. Guerra looked to be too far gone into a limbo of pain and lost pride to make any trouble, but there was no point to take chances. Not now. Not so close to finding Nolan again.

He followed Guerra down through the dark streets of Chihuahua. Off to the south, behind them, there was a blaze of activity as the *Federale* station burned away. Maybe, thought Azul, it will burn away the evidence. Maybe they'll think I went up with the flames. Or down.

He pushed on through the darkened streets, out past the plaza and out from the centre of Chihuahua. He saw the splintered pine Ramon Garcia had described, and smiled tightly as Guerra halted and looked both ways before turning right and leading the way up the side street.

It was a very quiet street. There were no dogs, nor any lights. Only high walls and fancy gates. The walls spread out a long way on both sides of the gates, and the houses beyond were invisible in the darkness. The night air smelled of orange blossom and money.

Guerra eased his horse up far enough down from one gate that they wouldn't be heard.

'That one,' he whispered. 'That's Nolan's place.'

'Good,' Azul whispered back. 'Go on in.'

'But I might be recognised,' said Guerra. 'What then?'

'Dead men don't spread stories,' said Azul.

Guerra took it the wrong way and rode towards the gate.

CHAPTER THIRTEEN

Raul Granos got back to the *hacienda* with a wagon-load of paper and a big smile on his handsome face.

He felt pleased with himself for bringing off what he considered a real coup: the purchase of enough high quality paper to print up around half a million dollars' worth of counterfeit notes, for only a little over his estimated price. He expected Nolan to share his delight. He was surprised that the dark man was so moody.

Over dinner, with half a bottle of tequila to bolster his courage, he mentioned it.

Nolan stared at him for a moment, then shook his head and said: 'I killed a man today. That Pinkerton who traced me up to Tucson. He showed up an' wanted a cut, so I got rid of him.'

'*Jesus y Maria!*' Raul crossed himself hurriedly. 'Why? Why a Pinkerton? He'll have left word. They'll come down here looking for us.'

'No.' Nolan shook his head. 'I don't think so.'

Raul stood up. 'I do. Those Pinkertons look after their own. If one found us here, then he'll have left a trail for others to follow.'

'Sit down.' Nolan's cold green eyes blazed. Granos sat down. 'I don't think they will. I don't think Carmady left any kind of trail, leastways, not down to here. Listen: if he planned to cut hisself in, he wasn't about to spread the news, right? If he was actin' on behalf o' the Pinkerton Agency, he'd've ridden in with a posse an' arrested me. He came alone. He said he wanted a share o' what we got because he knew all about it. Said he could use his contacts to clear the money fer us. That sound like a man about to make an arrest?'

Reluctantly Granos shook his head.

'So all he wanted was a share o' the proceeds,' continued Nolan. 'An' he thought he could get that by comin' up here an' bluffin' me out. Only he thought wrong. I called his bluff an' paid him in spades.'

'What happened?' Granos helped himself to whisky. 'How did you kill him?'

'Hit him on the head,' grinned Nolan, 'an' dumped him in the acid. Ain't nuthin' left now except a bag o' bones out in the garden.'

He chuckled at the memory. Granos swallowed hard and tried to quell his fear with liquor.

'Assumin' he was actin' off his own interests,' Nolan went on, 'he wouldn't have told anyone about us. Seein' that he wanted a cut, he was hardly likely to warn his people where we are. There could be a few folks around town saw him; maybe even knew he was lookin' fer us. It don't matter. We never saw him. He never came here. There ain't enough left to identify him, an' what there is would take a whole lotta findin'. So all we gotta do is sit tight an' print money.

'We're laughin' Mex. Laughin' all the way to the bank.'

Raul Granos shuddered some more and drank some whisky to calm the shaking. He nodded slowly, wondering what he had gotten himself mixed up in. The money side of it was fine – enough to tempt any man. But the money was leaving a long trail of killings behind, and Raul was a superstitious man; he counted ghosts. He counted eight so far. They began with the whore Nolan had killed; then there was Mrs Bixby and the brakeman on the train; the peace officer and his two deputies; the half-breed who had tried to stop them; now this new one, this Pinkerton. Raul crossed himself and poured a fresh drink. He didn't count Apaches.

'What's wrong?' Nolan's voice was cold and calm and spiteful. 'You scared?'

Raul nodded. 'Yes. I am. There are too many corpses marking our path.'

Nolan laughed out loud. 'Goddam Mex superstition! There ain't nuthin' behind us except dead men. An' they ain't tellin' nobody a thing.'

'I hope not,' said Raul. 'I hope not.'

Lieutenant Guerra rode up to the big gate and rattled the bars. A guard appeared, a man called Juan Ramirez. Guerra knew him, and Ramirez knew the *teniente*. He unlocked the gate and stepped inside the oiled swing of the iron, blocking it off from closing with his left foot.

'What is it?' He let his shotgun droop as he looked up at Guerra. 'Why come so late?'

The last word got choked off in the blood filling his mouth as Azul's knife sank deep into his windpipe. He dropped the shotgun and reached up, trying to pull the knife out. Azul shouldered Guerra's horse aside and wrenched the blade clear. He did it by pulling it away to the side, severing Ramirez's carotid artery. Blood fountained over the gatepost and the *pistolero* slumped to his knees. Azul caught him and shoved him back against the stonework so that he rested there as though asleep. Azul wiped the blade clean on the man's shirt and got his pony.

Guerra quietened the restive grey with automatic motions. His eyes were blank and dead. They looked even more dead than Ramirez's. The bruises on his face were in full flower by now, spreading dark shadows under his eyes in contrast to the pallor of his skin. His moustache drooped and he chewed nervously on the straggling ends. He resembled a nervous corpse.

'Let's go,' said Azul. 'One more guard an' you're free.'

'Never,' mumbled Guerra, 'I shall never be free. I have betrayed my duty. How can I be free after that?'

Abruptly, he slammed heels against the grey stallion and took off up the drive. Azul cursed and heeled the mustang in pursuit. The hooves made a loud sound on the sand.

Azul closed on the grey and swung the Winchester viciously at the animal's head. The stallion veered away, turning on to the grass. The hoofbeats got quieter. Azul guided the pinto with his knees, letting the reins fall clear. The mustang was Apache trained, which meant war-trained to ride down and cut out another horse. Azul needed only to stay on the plunging beast with both hands free to strike at his target. Guerra tried to turn the grey back in the direction of the house. The mustang cut it off, driving a shoulder against the stallion so that the larger horse checked and fought to alter its direction.

Azul came off the mustang's back in a wild dive. He dropped the Winchester as he felt his arms wrap around Guerra. Then he was tumbling down on to the parched grass.

The fall pained his ribs, but he ignored that hurt as he rolled over, clutching at the *Federale* officer.

Guerra punched him in the mouth. A weak blow. Azul concentrated on getting his hands where they could shut off Guerra's cries. He got one over the Mexican's lips, but Guerra bit him and kicked himself clear. Azul snarled and drew the Bowie knife.

He launched his body forwards with both arms stretched out in front. Guerra opened his mouth to scream a warning. The blade of the Bowie went in between his teeth and stuck deep into the back of his throat. His cry choked off and his teeth made a metallic clicking sound as they snapped shut on the razor-edged blade.

Azul drove it deeper, until the brass guard pressed up against Guerra's teeth.

'It's not a bullet,' he grunted, 'but bite it anyway.'

He yanked the blade sideways, cutting through Guerra's cheek as far as the jaw bone. The *teniente* was still trying to scream, so his tongue got sliced away and slid backwards down his throat. He began to choke. Azul tugged the knife loose and dropped his hand.

Guerra was on his knees with both hands pressed to his face. He was trying hard to hold his cheek together and cough up his swallowed tongue. He made a noise like an angry toad. Azul brought his arm up in a hard, sweeping curve. The point of the Bowie went in under Guerra's jaw. It drove up through the roof of his mouth and cut off his croaking. It went into the underside of his brain.

As abruptly as he had made his dash for freedom Guerra died. His eyes went suddenly blank and his hands fell down by his sides. A flap of skin hung loose along his jaw and his uniform got bloody.

Azul yanked the knife loose and pushed it back in the sheath. Guerra stayed upright for a moment, then folded back until his head rested on the grass behind his feet. His eyes stared up at the sky and his mouth began to fill with blood. It ran, thick and black in the moonlight, out of the cut along his face, trickling down into his hair and his ear, then dripping sluggishly on to the grass.

Azul turned, listening to the sounds of shouting from the house.

He heard men running towards him, saw the mustang waiting a few yards off. Like any well-trained Apache war-horse, the pinto was waiting for its rider to come back and remount. Azul ran towards it, stooped over. He reached the pony and slammed the flat of his hand hard against its rump. The mustang squealed a protest and kicked back, then took off at a fast gallop across the night-shaded grass.

Azul ran in the opposite direction.

A gun went off, exploding a brief flash that lit up two figures. Both ran after the panicked mustang. Azul moved away from them, making for the spread of a jacaranda tree close by the driveway.

He bellied down by the trunk, hugging shadow like a stalking wolf. There was light showing from the front of the house and more from the balcony. He crawled into another pool of shadow and paused, watching. There were two men on the balcony. One was a Mexican.

The other was Nolan.

Azul crawled on, then stood up as he saw Nolan and the other man move to the far end of the balcony. Bent low, he ran across the drive, angling up to cross it closer to the house. He ran from tree to tree, using the darkness with all the skill taught him in his Apache youth. He reached the house and threw himself flat alongside the raised porch. Somewhere behind him the mustang was still running and men were still firing guns, still shouting. He used the confusion to work his way round the side of the *hacienda* and kick a window in.

He climbed through and dropped to the floor.

There was a curious smell in the room, one he had never known before. He drew his Colt and crouched down in the darkness, waiting for his eyes to grow accustomed to the gloom. When he could see clearly again he stood up and looked around.

At the centre of the room was a spread of machinery that looked impressive and totally unrecognisable. It was surrounded by great vats of some black liquid and others that held a bad-smelling, colourless liquid. There were crates stacked around the machinery. One was open and he saw that it held paper. It was fine, crisp paper: the kind five dollar bills get printed on. Azul grinned. So this was where Nolan planned to make his fortune.

He went up to the far end of the lay-out, where there was a jig like the steam-presses he had seen in Chinese laundries, and a big, inky roller.

He ducked down, looking between the plates of the press.

Moonlight filtered in through the broken window. It shone on oiled metal. On two squares of oiled metal. Azul bent closer, peering at the etching of the plates. There was writing on them, but reversed; and the picture of a man's head.

Azul smiled, realising that these must be the stolen plates.

He holstered the Colt and drew the Bowie knife. He put the blade on the lower plate. It was hard metal, but the Bowie still left a long, thin line across the surface. He began to scrape. Up. Down. Across. When he was satisfied he reached up and set to scoring lines over the upper plate. When he was finished both pieces of metal were covered with a tracery of lines that cut through the engraved words, scoured the pictures. The plates were useless.

He heard voices outside, approaching the window. Two guards still alive, Nolan and Granos, and the servants . . . long odds in the enclosed space of the cellar. He reached up and grabbed a lantern from the ceiling. Smashed it over the machinery. He took another and hurled it down after the first. Then he grabbed two more and threw them against the crates of paper. The voices got closer. The cellar filled with the acrid reek of kerosene. He took more lanterns down and hurled them at random against workbenches. The voices fell silent. There was a pause. Then someone shouted in Mexican: 'There's a window broken. He must be in the cellar.' He took another lantern and tossed it against the wall beneath the window. The same voice yelled: 'I hear him! He's in there.'

A face showed, peering through the shattered frame.

Azul backed against the far wall, looking for a door.

The face went away and a hand poked in. It held a Colt's Peacemaker that bucked and spouted flame. The bullet ricochetted off the stone a yard to Azul's left. The muzzle flash ignited the kerosene dripping off the wall and window frame.

The gunman screamed as the kerosene ignited and withdrew his arm.

The fire spurted in a great circle, lighting a dark square where the empty window opened on to the night. Flame gusted out, driving back the guards. It ran down the wall and over the floor. It touched the kerosene dripping from the printing machinery and jumped upwards, hungry for fresh fuel. It found it on the trestles and inking vats, on the rollers and the press. It raced along the centre of the cellar and leapt across to the crated paper. Above the machinery, a lantern exploded, spreading glass and flame in a shrapnel burst of raw fire. The lanterns along the walls began to explode, adding still more kerosene to the blaze.

The paper began to burn. The vats of ink and acid, their glass containers held in wood or straw, began to flame. The heat cracked the glass and black rivulets of ink flowed thickly steaming over the stonework. The acid sizzled, filling the room with clogging fumes.

Azul felt his eyes water and his throat fill up with the stinking, nauseous gas. He choked and pressed his sleeve over his lips. Behind him a door opened.

He turned, levelling the Colt.

A man appeared in the doorway at the head of the stairs to Azul's right. He was the Mexican Azul had seen on the balcony. He wore tight black pants with big silver conchos down the sides, a tooled belt with fancy silver stitching, and a white shirt with wide sleeves and a big, rolling collar. He held a Winchester with silver studs in the stock making a snake pattern that matched the tooling on his belt. He was handsome, his black hair showing distinguished traces of grey at the temples. His mouth hung open and his eyes looked mad.

He ran down the stairs, yelling; oblivious of the half-breed snugged up against the wall.

Azul let him go by, then ran up the stairs and pulled the door shut. There was a lock with a key sticking out of the hole. He turned it and went looking for Nolan.

Raul Granos saw the blaze and tossed his Winchester to one side.

His equipment was burning! His beautiful equipment! The finest he had ever owned. It was worth every rotten *peseta* of Nolan's stolen money. He had given up his little press and his little office in the Calle Vizcada for this . . .

. . . For this and the promise of a fortune.

And now it burned.

It burned from end to end. The paper Raul had bought so carefully was ablaze. The rubber matting of the press beds was ablaze. The inking rollers were ablaze. The pressing beds themselves were ablaze.

Raul Granos ran down the cellar. He felt no pain as sparks flamed in his hair. He was unconscious of the little flickers that ran up his legs as he splashed burning kerosene over his pants. Some automatic defence caused him to hold his breath against the fumes of acid.

He reached the flatbeds of the press and moaned. They were covered in flame. His hands burned as he tried to tug the plates loose. The pain forced him back.

He stared at the burning, dripping plates and regretted the day he had decided to ride up to Tucson in search of a fortune.

He remembered a sermon he had once heard in the church at the south end of Chihuahua. He had gone there as he always did – not for any religious reason, but because he got more orders, more work, by showing his face there and listening to the *padre* announcing births and deaths and marriages. Afterwards he would approach the people mentioned and suggest a modest notice – printed out by Raul Granos, of course, – to appear in the paper, or on walls; or wherever money could be made.

Love of money is the root of all evil . . .

That was what the *padre* had said that day.

There are greater rewards in heaven. To love your fellow man above yourself, that is the greater love. The saving grace. To love money is easy. To forsake that love and give it over to those who need is the hard thing . . .

Raul had laughed at the stupid sentiment. Then. Not now.

Not with his beautiful machinery, his beautiful

dreams, dying around him. Dying in a raging welter of flame.

He was suddenly aware of the danger.

The whole cellar was blazing. The lanterns were lit brighter than ever intended and there was acid and ink spilling over the floor; paper aflame; woodwork. All of it. The dream was dead and burned.

He had to get out.

He was suddenly aware of the cloying fumes of spilled and heated acid burning his eyes and mouth.

He looked down the cellar. To the right was a solid wall of flame: impassable.

To the left, the fire seemed thinner. Raul Granos tried to go that way. He had to pass a spilled vat of acid to do it, and when he held his breath and stumbled past the vat, he lost his sense of direction as his eyes watered and closed.

He opened them again when he thought he was past. They stung so badly he wiped at them and moaned with the pain of the wiping. He staggered on. Tripped. His face hit the floor and burned. He opened his eyes and rolled away as he felt his lashes burn. He screamed as he put his right hand down into a pool of burning kerosene. He rolled back and screamed again as acid splashed against his face. He fought his own numb body to get upright and stagger onwards. Then he hit a crate and fell flat on his face with burning paper cascading over his sprawled body.

He pushed clear, climbing on to hands and knees.

He couldn't see anymore and he was fighting to breathe. He could still feel the pain of the flames licking around his body, but they didn't seem to matter all that much. What he had to do was get upright. Stand up and get to the stairs. Get up the stairs and out into the *hacienda*. Nolan would look after him.

Yes . . . Nolan would look after him. The dark man needed him. Needed Raul Granos to print the money . . .

. . . But there wasn't money anymore. It was gone. Melted. Burned.

Raul climbed to his feet and stumbled through the fire. His hair took flame and began to drop burning waves over his shoulders. His shirt and pants smouldered. His hands were raw, blistered and cracking like frying pork. His face was a scorched mask devoid of hair, the flesh puffing up and splitting with the sizzle of juices and blood as they poured from the blisters.

The acid fumes filled his eyes and puffed them closed. His throat got thick, so thick he couldn't even scream anymore.

Raul Granos lost his direction entirely and stumbled back into the flames. A section of woodwork collapsed over him, driving him down against the flame-lapped stonework of the floor. He wriggled loose and tottered down the cellar. His clothes were blazing. His hair. His face. He was a stumbling, mad, corpse.

He got back to the big press and laughed. It was an eery, ugly sound, because it came up out of lungs poisoned by the acid and fire, through a throat burned dry by flame and past lips that were cracked and roasted. He thrust his hands into the press and laughed again as molten metal dripped on to his blackened flesh.

Then he fell down and burned alongside his press.

Azul locked the cellar door and went looking for Nolan.

He was on the ground floor of the *hacienda*, with a narrow corridor behind him and a big, wood door in front.

He checked the rear of the corridor first: it opened into the kitchen.

A fat lady with greasy hair twisted into long plaits that framed two wide, frightened eyes waved a meat cleaver in his direction. Behind her stood a slender girl with even bigger eyes. She was holding a long-bladed carving knife in both trembling hands. Farther back, poised midway between a pine dresser and the door, was a stoop-shouldered man with dark eyes that managed to look more tired than scared. His hands were occupied with a bottle of mescal.

‘Get out,’ said Azul. ‘Get out while you can. The house is burning.’

‘Who are you?’ said the woman. ‘Why should we trust you?’

‘I am Azul,’ he said. ‘Some people call me Breed.’

‘Oh! Madre de Dios!’ The woman dropped her cleaver and crossed herself. *‘El Lobo! Es el tiempo de lobo! Vamanos!’*

She gathered up her skirts and essayed a run out of the kitchen, shoving the girl before her. The man got the door open and was long gone as the woman and the girl shuffled quickly away. Azul shut the door behind them and slid the bolts home. Then he turned back to the corridor outside.

He kicked the big oak door open and found himself in a wide, carpeted room with a huge fireplace and chairs of grainy cowhide spread over teak frames littered around the carpets and polished pine of the floor. To his right, where the door opened into the room, was a wide stairway. There was a big door facing him from across the room. It was open. He ran over and swung it shut. He dropped the heavy crossbar into place and turned the key in the lock. Then he tossed the key into the fireplace and raked burning logs clear of the grate, kicking them over the floor and the carpets, under the furniture.

The room began to fill with the smell of burning.

Azul went up the stairs.

A figure showed at the top, staring in amazement at the spreading blaze below. He was a Mexican, dressed in flare-bottomed pants and a big sombrero. He had a pistol belted around his waist and two wide bandoleers across his chest. He carried a shotgun.

He pointed the shotgun down the stairs and squeezed both barrels off together.

Azul dropped flat. He heard the thunder of the scattergun and felt air stir above him, the fire of pellets along his back and legs. He stuck his right arm out, pointing the Colt upwards, and squeezed the trigger.

From that position he had no hope of firing a killing

shot: he was too low down, and unsighted. The hit was lucky: it gave him time.

It caught the Mexican between his legs, hitting him in the right side of his inner thigh so that he yelped and reached down to clutch between his legs. Azul shifted, bringing the Colt up to snap a shot off as the man bent over. The bullet hit his descending face, entering through the left eye socket to emerge from the back of his neck. It opened his windpipe and broke his jaw, taking with it a fragment of spinal bone. The Mexican grunted and tumbled down the stairs into the flames.

Azul climbed to his feet and moved on upwards.

He got on to the landing and looked around. There were several doors opening off the walkway, but he had no means of telling where Nolan was. Not unless he took a chance.

He made his choice and opened his mouth.

'Nolan! Where are you? Nolan!'

A door at the eastern end of the landing opened and Azul spun round. He fired as he turned, off the hip, triggering twice: once dead; twice, safe.

A Mexican coughed blood and dropped a shotgun as he pressed hands to the hole in his belly. He fell down on to his knees and stared at Azul with wide, pain-glazed eyes. Blood ran out from between his fingers. It showed on the wall behind him. He spat and stretched his right arm out, trying to grasp the shotgun without moving his stomach or the hand holding his guts in.

Azul ran towards him and stamped a foot down over the clutching hand. The Mexican mouthed a curse and spat more blood over his shirt. Azul kicked him in the face and picked up the shotgun. It was a Meteor, with both barrels loaded on ten-gauge shot. The Mexican groaned and rolled on to his back. His hand fell away from his belly and irridescent bubbles frothed around the corners of his mouth. His stomach heaved, expelling a gust of air and a gout of blood. Then he lay still.

Azul glanced down at the room below.

The logs he had kicked over the floor had taken firm

hold, igniting the furniture and the carpets. The drapes along the walls and the flooring itself were burning. Smoke poured from the cellar, spreading a stinking miasma of acid and ink in heavy clouds through the burning gaps in the cellar door.

He ducked into the nearest room, swinging the shotgun in a traversing sweep across the empty scene. He worked his way along the landing, ignoring the danger of the fire as he checked one room after the other.

He got to the western end of the *hacienda* and kicked the last door open.

The room was obviously in use. The bed was neatly turned down, and a bottle of whisky stood on a side table, flanked by a clean glass. There was a black stetson hung off the foot of the brass bed, and a freshly-polished pair of black boots set up against the wall.

Azul ducked inside and opened the wardrobe. There was a black suit hanging there and a set of well-worn saddlebags on the floor. He kicked the door shut and checked the window. It was closed. He went back towards the door, almost falling over a ruckle in the carpet. When he looked down, he saw that the rug was drawn back from under the bed, one corner folded over to expose a length of planking with darker shadows showing between two boards than was normal.

He cocked both hammers of the Meteor and set the gun down on the bed. Then he drew his Bowie knife and worked it between two of the boards. One lifted easily. He tore it loose and lifted the other. There was a sack shoved down under the floor. He tugged it clear and pulled the neck open. The sack was full of money; more money than he had ever seen. There was a brass badge and a small revolver in the cache. He recognised them both. The last time he had seen them, they had been worn by Carmady. He tucked the badge into his vest and tossed the gun across the room. Then he picked up the sack of money and rose to his feet. Holding the scattergun at waist height he turned towards the door.

Smoke was beginning to spill up the stairs, the flames

getting a grip on the woodwork so that a solid sheet of fire covered the lower part. The glare outlined the man standing in the doorway. He held a Colt's Frontier model in his hand and an ugly smile on his face.

'Christ!' he said. 'I thought you was killed.'

The voice was flat and cold, only faintly tinged with surprise. It belonged to Nolan.

Azul felt a sudden chill run through him. Not that chill that comes with shock, or fear, but the awful, cold stillness of pent-up rage, the momentary calm that precedes the breaking of a storm.

'It's been a long time.' His voice was as cold as Nolan's, husky with hate. 'I'll enjoy killing you.'

Nolan went on smiling. He held his gun levelled on Azul's chest, his green eyes taking in the half-breed's face and the shotgun. It was as if both men were caught in stasis, time frozen so that the instant stretched out and pinned them down; immobile, waiting. One part of Azul's mind screamed out to pull the triggers of the scattergun and end it. To blast Nolan away; wipe out the long-held debt. Another part – the Apache part – told him to wait: Nolan should die slowly and in pain.

'Looks like a Mexican stand-off,' said Nolan. 'What we gonna do about it?'

'Why ask?' rasped Azul. 'You know I'll kill you.'

'You ain't so far.' Nolan seemed, almost, as though he wanted to talk. 'I know you want to kill me slow, so you ain't likely to use that shotgun. If you did – I could still down you. Like I said: it's a stand-off.'

Both guns held steady as the two men tensed, waiting for the moment when the other might relax a fraction and grant that vital instant's opening. They used words like knives, seeking to jar one another off guard.

'I got your money.' Azul let the sack drop to the floor between them. 'I finished your printing operation. You're back where you started. With nothing.'

'I had me a good time, though,' said Nolan. 'I settled an old score with yore father.'

Somewhere in the bowels of the house a vat of acid,

heated to bursting point, exploded with a dull echo. On the stairs, the fire crept higher, working its way towards the balcony.

'You'll die for it,' said Azul. 'You'll pay.'

Nolan smiled some more. He didn't seem to care about dying very much. He reminded Azul of another man he had seen, a long time ago. Azul, Sees-The-Fox, and a few other warriors had ridden on to the Llano Estacado in search of mustangs. They had been jumped by a scouting party of Comanche, outnumbering the Chiricahua by fourteen to six. The Apaches had run and forted up on a mesa. Azul had noticed that one of the Comanche took more chances than the others; his face was painted a uniform black, with a single red line painted on from hairline to jaw.

The death face, old Sees-The-Fox had told him, *it means he is committed to dying in battle. He must have lost someone dear to him, or maybe disgraced himself. He has decided that the only way he can make amends is to die. Men are like that sometimes. They forget that living is so much better than dying, and often harder. A man hopes to die well, but to die intentionally is madness.*

Soon after that, the Comanche had charged the mesa single-handed. He went down with three arrows and two bullets in his chest. Azul had seen him smile as he died. His fellow warriors had waited around for two days, mounting desultory attacks, then ridden off and let the Apaches go free.

Somehow, Nolan reminded Azul of that black painted warrior.

'Why do you keep my father's scalp?' he asked.

'I thought that might get to you.' Nolan laughed and reached inside his jacket with his left hand. 'I'll tell you about it.'

He tugged the scalp out and held it at arm's length. Then he tossed it on to the sacks of money. Azul started, his eyes wavering towards the hank of pale hair.

Nolan fired.

Azul sensed the movement of his trigger finger, or saw some minute alteration in the dark man's stance, or a subtle change in the ugly smile. He threw himself sideways and back, triggering the shotgun as he fell. He dropped the sights deliberately, hoping to catch Nolan in the legs, to leave the man alive for the longer, slower pleasures of Apache death.

Fire burned over his ribs and he heard Nolan's shot blast into the stonework of the wall behind him. At the same time, he saw the dark man twist back, hurling himself outwards through the door on to the balcony beyond.

Nolan's bullet had scored a bloody line through the bandages on Azul's stomach. The bullet had cut flesh, but nothing else. As he fell, Azul noticed that Nolan's right leg was peppered with shot, though most of the charge had only splintered wood from the doorframe.

He threw the scattergun away and drew his Colt. He kicked the sacks of money and the scalp up against his chest and shoved them over the side of the room as he huddled back against the wall. Nolan's gun blew chips from the foot of the bed. A second shot ploughed splinters from the floor. Azul grabbed his father's scalp and shoved it inside his shirt. He fired blind through the empty doorway.

'You missed!' shouted Nolan. 'You need to shoot better to catch me.'

'Yeah?' Azul snarled back. 'Catch this.'

He picked up the sack of money and pitched it out through the door, up high, so that it flew across the balcony and landed on the steps beyond.

The sack hit four treads from the top. Then it rolled another three and came to rest hanging over the eighth. The flames were already sputtering along the seventh step. The flames flickered up and took hold on the burlap. The sack began to burn.

'You goddam bastard!' Nolan fired through the door. 'That's my money!'

He fired again and powered into a wild dive that took

him past the doorway and rolling down the stairs. He dropped the Colt as he reached for the sack, ignoring the flames that scorched his hands and face. He got hold of the sack and twisted round, crabbing back up the stairs as he drew the Remington Star from his hideaway holster.

Azul came out of the bedroom with the Colt cocked and pointed out. He slid across the balcony and thrust his arm out through the rail to angle round on Nolan. He fired. Nolan cursed as the bullet sharded plaster over his face. He fired blind, blinking to clear the dust from his eyes. Azul fired again, aiming carefully.

It was a difficult shot, because he was twisted over on his side and his ribs were hurting. He had his right arm stuck out through the wooden rails of the balcony and there was smoke and flame lifting up from the room below that made his eyes smart. It was a good shot. It hit exactly where he aimed. It hit the .38 pistol in Nolan's hand and tore it loose.

The Remington spun free and tumbled back into the blaze. Almost immediately, the magazine began to detonate and the sharp explosions of the cartridges made a counterpoint to the duller roar of the fire and the distant, echoing blasts of exploding vats.

'Get up.' Azul climbed to his feet with the Colt levelled on Nolan's face. 'Get up and pay your debts.'

Nolan shrugged and climbed the stairs. He slapped flame from the burlap sack, then looked at Azul.

'I guess you want this.'

'No,' grunted the half-breed. 'Throw it away. Into the fire.'

He waited for Nolan to obey the order.

'You're crazy. You must be. Pure *loco*!'

'Throw it,' said Azul. 'Easy come, easy go.'

'Yeah,' said Nolan. 'A whore told me that once.'

But he still tossed the sack out into the flames that were consuming the *hacienda*.

CHAPTER FOURTEEN

Azul glanced round, looking for a way out.

The stairway and the room below were a furnace. The ceiling was beginning to burn and ominous streamers of smoke drifted up from the planking of the balcony. He could hear the animals in the stable behind the *hacienda* screaming as they scented the fire. There was a door at the western end of the balcony. Azul shouted over the sound of the fire, calling for Nolan to lead the way out. He stayed back behind the scalp-hunter, out of arm's reach.

Nolan grinned and made for the door. His expression disturbed Azul: it was too calm, too assured.

Nolan opened the door. It swung out on well-oiled hinges, giving access to the outer balcony. When it opened, the heated air of the burning room swirled and rushed towards the cold of the night. There was a sudden blast of heat and a skirling cloud of smoke that washed around Azul. He coughed. Nolan threw himself forwards, slamming the door back in the half-breed's face.

Azul caught it on his left shoulder and drove his weight against it.

The door swung back and he powered through into Nolan's swinging fist.

The blow landed solidly in his face, mashing his lips against his teeth so that he staggered, his eyes watering. In the same instant Nolan grabbed his wrist and twisted his arm forwards and round, pivoting on one foot to drive a knee up into Azul's groin.

Azul felt the pain flood through his belly, nausea and hate curdling together in his throat. Involuntarily, he doubled over, his pained muscles reacting instinctively to the kick.

He pushed forwards, wrapping his left arm around Nolan's leg as the dark man moved to kick again. He pulled the leg up close to his chest and rammed his head into the man's lower belly. Nolan grunted. Azul felt his balance go and tugged Nolan down on top of him.

Nolan was still holding on to his wrist, and Azul could feel the tension in the joints of his elbow and shoulder as his arm bent round. His left arm was pinned under his body and Nolan was twisting his right up behind his back. Azul hammered his forehead against Nolan's stomach. The scalphunter twisted, wrapping his legs about Azul's waist and squeezing hard. Azul felt his fingers opening, forced loose from the Colt by the pressure of Nolan's grip.

He tried to fire the pistol, but his thumb was pulled away from the hammer and his trigger finger slid loose from the guard. The gun fell out of his hand, thudding on to the boards of the balcony.

Nolan let go of his wrist, turning as he reached for the gun. Azul heaved up, twisting over so that their interlocked bodies rolled, covering the pistol. Nolan grabbed his hair and yanked his head back and hammered a blow into his face. Azul got his left arm free and rammed his palm under Nolan's chin. The blow snapped the scalphunter's head up and back and Azul sank his fingers into the skin of the cheeks and lips and pushed. His nails dug deep into flesh and Nolan was forced backwards, his spine arcing as the half-breed reached down with his right hand, trying to get it round the hilt of the knife tucked into his moccasin.

Azul's fingers touched the haft, but then Nolan rolled and sprang his legs loose. At the same time, he clapped the heels of both hands against the sides of Azul's neck. The blow sent a massive, numbing shock through the nerves connecting neck to brain. Azul's mouth jumped open and bright light exploded through his eyes. For a moment he was blind, his body frozen. Nolan rolled loose, scrabbling for the Colt.

Instinct, rather than consciousness, dictated Azul's movements.

He got the throwing knife free and swung it up and across as he twisted over to where he sensed Nolan should be. His left arm swept out in a flat arc, fingers stiffened. He felt that hand strike soft flesh and heard Nolan grunt, then the knife cut through cloth and he was over the scalphunter's body.

Nolan felt his wrist go numb as the sweeping hand smashed it clear of the Colt. Then pain lanced his neck as the blade sliced a red line under his chin.

Azul saw the Colt and swung a leg to kick the gun away. It slid out across the balcony and hung for a moment, balanced on the edge. Then it fell from sight. He was slicing the knife back down towards Nolan's face when the scalphunter lifted both his legs and rammed them against the small of the half-breed's back. The blow was sufficiently powerful to lift Azul up, throwing him against the wall of the balcony. Agony danced over his damaged ribs and his face hit the rails with stunning force. He felt his lips split and blood spurt from his nose.

He spat as he turned, still holding the knife.

Nolan was out of range, crabbing backwards with the Bowie in his left hand. Azul checked the sheath: the leather was empty.

He rolled over and came up on his feet. Nolan rose at the same time. He held the Bowie knife out in front of his body, thumb rested up against the guard so that the longer edge, the cutting edge, was uppermost. He held it out at arm's length, his knees bent and his left arm extended forwards and slightly to the side.

Azul recognised the stance of an experienced knife fighter. He matched it, weighing the odds, looking for an opening.

The Bowie was around nine inches long in the blade,

tapering down from a two-inch tang to a needle point. The topside of the blade was flat, close on a half inch thick. After that, it tapered thinner to the curve of the overside. That curve and two inches more were honed fine; sharp enough to shave with. The throwing knife was straight-bladed, seven inches from tang to point. It was one inch wide at the guard, flaring slightly towards the tip, where the leaf-shaped blade fanned out over an inch and a half before closing down to the fine, needle-tipped point. It was razor-sharp on both sides. But there was no guard to catch incoming blows, and it lacked the weight and the length of the Bowie.

Nolan held the advantage.

In knife fighting there are two styles. One consists of using weight and cutting power to wear down the opponent and slap his blade away, using your own, at the same time, to carve his flesh. The other depends on speed – like using a rapier, rather than a sabre – to dart in and stab, cut, then get clear fast enough to avoid the other man's thrust. In a sword fight, the man with the rapier will usually win because he moves faster and needs only one firm blow to kill. That demands space; room to move in. Knife fighting is different. Both men are close – have to be to strike – so the darting, balletic movements of the finer blade get lost under the sheer weight of the heavier weapon.

Azul knew that he was on the losing side.

Unless he took a long shot. But he wasn't quite ready for that. Yet.

A man with a throwing knife always has one advantage over a man with a Bowie: he can throw his blade. It's so obvious that most people forget it, or if they think about it, they overlook the problems.

It's usage depends on skill and long practice. To throw a knife requires a different stance to fighting with it, calls for a change of position that might afford an opening. The thrown knife may go in over the other man's guard and kill him if it's placed right. But the other man is moving around, and he can move fast enough to deflect the thrown blade. Or it might hit his arm, or leg, or some other place that won't hamper him too much while he steps in and cuts the thrower to pieces.

Azul backed up and waited for Nolan to come to him. He held the knife loose in his right hand, ready to use the blade to turn Nolan's thrust, or to flip it over and throw it into the scalphunter's body.

Nolan grinned and moved forwards on cat's feet, the Bowie shifting back and forth before him. Azul cut inwards. Took the blade on his own knife and turned it out. He sliced the thinner knife at Nolan's stomach, but the Bowie swung back and snatched the edge away. Azul sprang back from the point.

Nolan cut again. Azul lifted the throwing knife to block off the swing. The Bowie hit and smashed the blade aside. Nolan thrust forwards, angling for the chest. Azul twisted, hiking his left arm back behind him as the Bowie scored a crimson line over the left side of his chest. He cut in, but Nolan's left arm blocked his stroke, shoving the knife out and down as the scalphunter reversed his swing to shunt the Bowie up towards Azul's ribs.

Azul blocked the stab with his left forearm. He felt the Bowie slice flesh as Nolan heaved it up and back.

He cut out and forwards, slicing at Nolan's face. The scalphunter took the blow on his left forearm, ducking down to ram the Bowie at Azul's stomach. The half-breed sucked his stomach in, pivoting sideways so that the thrusting blade stroked over his ribs and he could bring his left arm down to trap Nolan's knife against his side.

He twisted, looping his right down to cut at Nolan's ribs as he pulled the dark man towards him, spinning him off balance so that Nolan fell towards him, fighting to tug his arm loose from Azul's grip. Azul brought the knife down under Nolan's arm. It cut into cloth and snagged on the shoulder-holster. Nolan swung his left arm, punching at Azul's head. The blow stung Azul's ear, knocking him sideways.

Nolan pulled his arm free and jumped back. He turned the Bowie as he moved, cutting over Azul's side.

Azul lurched away.

Nolan stepped farther back, regaining balance. He fetched up against the door, leaning one shoulder on the woodwork as he panted and fought to gain his breath. His left hand went down on to the catch. Azul moved forwards, poised on the balls of his feet, knife held out ready to cut up into Nolan's ribs.

Nolan turned the catch. He eased back, swinging the door out from the frame. His hand closed over the edge and he poised, waiting. Azul closed on him and Nolan feigned a groan, letting his knife hand droop. Azul powered forwards. Nolan swung the door all the way open, smashing it into the half-breed's path. It hit Azul along the right side of his face. His knife dug into the woodwork and blood spurted from his nose and mouth. Nolan hefted the Bowie sideways in a savage cut. Azul ducked, feeling the blade slice hair from his scalp. He yanked the throwing knife out of the wood and lifted his left arm as he went back, off balance.

Nolan heaved the door open again and jumped inside. He swung it shut as Azul came towards him, smashing it back against the out-thrust arm.

The stairway was now a blazing pyre, fed by the incandescence of the room below. Flame licked along the balcony, sparking bright off of the rugs and wicker hung on the walls. The plasterwork was getting black, cracking and peeling where the flames licked upwards to lap against the ceiling. Nolan ran into the bedroom. The stable was directly below: if he could get out of the window and drop down before the crazy 'breed reached him, he could maybe get away.

Azul lifted his sleeve up and wiped the blood from his mouth and nose. Then he swung the door open and went through.

Heat hit him like a solid wall. He felt his hair crackle

and singe as he raced across the balcony. He saw Nolan lifting the window and reacted on pure instinct.

His right arm lifted up over and behind his head. The throwing knife slipped over from shaft to blade with the reflex action of hate and practice and rage. His arm swung out, fingers opening to release the blade. It spun away and glinted through the heated air. It turned over and over, shafting light like a thunderbolt. It hit Nolan high up on his right shoulder. The tip hit the bone of his clavicle and cut the muscle. Nolan's arm bounced free of the window as the knife bounced from his back.

The scalphunter yelled and swung the Bowie round. His eyes were mad and he charged across the room with the big blade held out in front like a bayonet. Azul ducked sideways.

Nolan went out through the door screaming, stumbling on to the balcony with the knife still stuck out in front of him and a long, lonesome wail screaming from between his parted lips.

Azul went over and picked up the throwing knife. There was blood all over the tip. He lifted it and paced out towards the door.

When he got it open he saw Nolan tugging at the door on to the outer balcony. The house was burning, great chunks of the ceiling falling down into the fire below as the heat broke slabs of plaster loose and dropped them down into the blaze. They hit with dull, *crumping* sounds, showering spires of sparks up through the blazing air.

Nolan shouted and turned away from the door.

Azul had no way of knowing whether it was locked, or if the scalphunter had succumbed to total madness.

Nolan ran towards him. He swung the Bowie in a wild curve that forced Azul to jump back, glancing the blade off the thinner knife. Azul moved away, swinging his own blade in an unsweeping curve that sliced Nolan's face from jaw to hairline.

The cut went in on the underside of Nolan's jaw, lifting up over his cheek to where the cheekbone stuck out below his eye socket. The tip of Azul's knife struck hard against teeth, then grated on over bone and sliced deep into the ball of the eye itself. It sliced upwards through the soft pupil and cut through the bony ridge above. It scored a wide-lipped line over Nolan's forehead, riding upwards into the hair.

Blood spurted out over Nolan's face and he screamed again, dropping the Bowie as he pressed burned hands to his wasted face.

Azul swung away, turning to thrust the knife into Nolan's ribs.

But the dark man went on screaming and kicked the blade aside as he lurched over the balcony into the flames below.

His falling body lifted up a great cloud of sparks as he crashed through the woodwork. He was still screaming as he hit the floor and bounced into the fire. He went on screaming as Azul stood up and turned away, looking for a way out.

The half-breed went back inside the bedroom and opened the window. There was the shiny roof of a tiled outhouse below him, and he swung through and dropped down on to the slanting roof. He slid, and tumbled off the lower rim, falling out into a yard filled with nervous horses.

When he got back on his feet he saw that one of the stamping ponies was the black Nolan had taken away from the train. He stood up and sank a hand into the stallion's mane, dragging the big head down until he got the horse calmed. Then he eased it back towards the stable and found a saddle; fought the leather on to the nervous beast.

Sparks were falling over the stable as flame guttered from the windows of the house. And the sound of shouting and the clang of firebuckets came up from the side-streets leading down into Chihuahua. The *hacienda* was in full flame, gouts like the withered arms of old men reaching out through the windows, sharp breaths of livid fire gusting skywards through roof and walls. Azul took the black horse out into the open then went back to free the other animals.

They came out like corks from shaken bottles, bursting into the night with their heads down and legs pumping, blind to the men trying to halt them, intent only on breaking free, away from the fire and the guns; away from the stench of death and burning.

Azul went with them. He crouched down in the saddle and heeled the big black horse towards the front gate. He followed the others through, bursting out into the street beyond as men jumped aside and hollered vague resistance to the rush of horses.

Azul stayed with the run until it reached the centre of Chihuahua, then he peeled off and turned the black horse north. There was a bright light in the sky behind him, flame lapping up to greet the stars as Nolan's house burned down. Few people paid any attention to the tall man on the black horse and in a while Azul stopped and cleaned his face. There was a water trough built up against a big stone wall, spilling over with fresh spring water. It felt good on his skin, washing away the blood and soot and some of the pain. His ribs ached and his mouth felt raw. His nose continued to bleed slightly and the cuts along his chest and arms stung. But he felt good. Felt better than he had thought was possible, better than he had felt in a long time.

Nolan was dead. Had to be. Nothing could survive that fire.

The scalphunter was burning now. His skin would blister and crack, blacken, burn. His hair would take flame and when he tried to breathe all he would taste would be the agony of intaken heat.

Azul savoured the thought, and a slow smile spread across his bruised, bloody face. He reached inside his shirt and touched the hank of hair that was all now left of his father. He would take it back to the sierra Mogallon, to the high place where once his *rancheria* had stood, to the place where the bones of his parents rested, to his birth tree. He would leave the hair there, up in the lonely fastness of the high country, the Apache country. And perhaps his father and mother would see it done and smile on the son.

He drank, relishing the coolness, then pulled back his sleeve and stared at the oath scars showing white through the tan of his left arm. He touched the puckered flesh and looked to where light shone against the night sky.

Nolan was dead.

Azul's only regret was that he couldn't watch.

CHAPTER FIFTEEN

The volunteer firefighters were tired. They had already doused the blaze that threatened to consume the *Federale* station and spread out into the streets. The bodies they found had made them nervous: there was something evil afoot this night. The second blaze proved it.

They were shocked to find Juan Ramirez and Lieutenant Guerra dead outside the *yanqui*'s house and they crossed themselves and made the sign that wards off evil when they saw how the throats were ripped out. It was as though some blood-mad beast had torn the men to spill their blood so wantonly. They hoped the fire would consume whatever monster had done these awful things as it consumed the *hacienda*, for – surely – there was nothing they could do. The place was too far gone for bucket chains, or even the new, hand-operated pump, to be any good. All they could do was watch and take care that the blaze didn't spread.

They were horrified when something came out of the flames.

It had the dimensions of a man, but it was a creation of hell. It screamed and waved blazing arms that scattered gobbets of sizzling blood as it stumbled towards them.

One, braver than his fellows, or perhaps less religious, hurled a bucket of water over the creature and beat it down on to the ground while another threw a blanket over it and slapped the flames out.

The *padre* ran up then and began to administer the last rites, seeing that the thing was a man, and dying.

The thing stopped him. It lifted a hand that was hideously burned and opened one eye. The other was blind, torn apart as though a claw had raked over the eye socket and sliced through the pulpy softness of the ball. Its lips were blackened and crusted with boils, and the voice was harsh, as if the fires of hell had scorched the lungs and throat.

'I ain't dyin'.' It said. 'Get me fixed up. I got someone to kill.'

The eye closed and the thing slumped back, wheezing gasps spitting blood over the maimed chin. The priest called for men to get a blanket under it and carry it down to the church. They thought it would be better to let it die because it was wrong and obviously had no chance of living, but they did what the priest told them and carried it back and set it down in the *padre*'s own room where the old woman who looked after him cut the clothes away from the thing and set to applying ointments to the body. She was part-Indian, a Yaqui, baptised into the Christian faith, but retaining her old skills with medicines and salves. She kept the thing alive.

But it never thanked her.

All it said during the long months of nursing was 'Save me. I got someone to kill.'

Azul rode northwards in the direction of Tres Castillos. After that he swung in a westerly direction, skirting round Carrizal and the north flank of the Candelarias heading up towards Lake Guzman. He stayed away from the towns because he knew the *Federales* would be looking for him with renewed vigour. He went around the lake and rode along the river for a while, then the Casas Grandes faded away behind him and he came up to the border. He crossed over where the country was empty of anything but Apaches and animals. He steered on a line that went north between Lordsburg and Deming, moving up past Silver City and what was left of Santa Rita del Cobre, towards the Pinos Altos and the high fork of the Gila.

After that he rode hard for the Mogallons.

It was cold up in the high mountains. Winter was settling down and freezing the water; the grass was dry and dead. Like the cold, bleak place where his *rancheria* had once been.

He stopped there and sat for a long time; remembering. The hogans were gone, and the horses, and the dogs. And the people. It was a dead place. A place of death and memories. Grass had sprung up and withered where the lodges had been. He shivered, feeling frost coat his hair and face. There were gopher holes dug down into the ground, and the tiny prairie dogs squealed and stared at the intruder.

When the sun came up and warmed him a little he rose to his feet and mounted the big black horse. He rode out to the high and lonely place where his father had taken him and, hand-in-hand with his mother, showed him his birth tree.

He took the scalp out of his shirt and hung it on the tree. The old piñon was stark, bare of leaves. The dry, withered branches rustled in the winter wind like the voices of old men; or the gentle, tumultuous whisperings of dead memories. The wind caught the hair and spread it out, gusting through the branches so that the dry, dead hair fluttered in long streamers that reflected the pale sunlight from the silvery strands.

Azul stood silent, watching the hair drift in the wind.

Up on the higher faces of the rock a wolf howled. Azul wondered why it called so late in the day. Then he remembered something Sees-Both-Ways, the shaman, had told.

There is a balance in life that is in all men, all things. It is a part of us, and it binds us to everything around us. It is in the wolf and the vulture. In the man and the cactus. It is everywhere; it is the world. The man who forgets that, forgets what he is and becomes nothing. The echo of death sounds in all ears; the echo of life is the new sound you hear in your mind. The two belong together.

Azul squatted down and watched the wolf come close. It was a big, grey lobo with pale yellow eyes and the gaunt flanks of early winter marking the hardness of its life. It hunkered down and watched him from a safe distance, not sure that he was alive and unwilling to risk an attack.

It stayed there until the sun lifted up to the middle of the sky and Azul stood up. Then it turned and ran out into the rocks.

'Wolf,' said Azul quietly, 'I will go and kill a deer for you. I shall kill it and bring it back here, to where you can guard the tree.'

He kept his promise.

THE END

Don't miss the first book in the GUNSLINGER SERIES

THE MASSACRE TRIAL

Charles C. Garrett

RYKER KNOWS GUNS LIKE OTHER MEN KNOW HOW TO BREATHE . . .

John Ryker was a gunsmith. One of the best at a time when speed and skill with a shooting iron were as vital to survival as food in your belly.

Then one day Ryker sold a man a gun – a Deringer – that later killed a President. That incident set Ryker on a vengeance trail of blood and conflict, for the gunsmith became The Gunslinger – a man whose expertise with all the weapons of the West made him the most lethal fighting and killing force in a violent land . . .

In the books of the *Gunslinger* series, authentic details of the guns of the West are combined with vivid and bloody action to produce one of the best Western sagas ever published.